[signature]

ANTHONY RYAN

A PILGRIMAGE OF SWORDS

THE SEVEN SWORDS
BOOK ONE

Anthony Ryan

Subterranean Press • 2019

First Edition

ISBN
978-1-59606-924-4

Subterranean Press
PO Box 190106
Burton, MI 48519

subterraneanpress.com

Manufactured in the United States of America

This story is dedicated to the late, great Ray Harryhausen—filmmaker, animator and true magician who crafted many wonders to light my childhood imagination and continues to provide a well of inspiration, for this tale and many others.

The Whisp

The Crescent

Crucible
Bridge

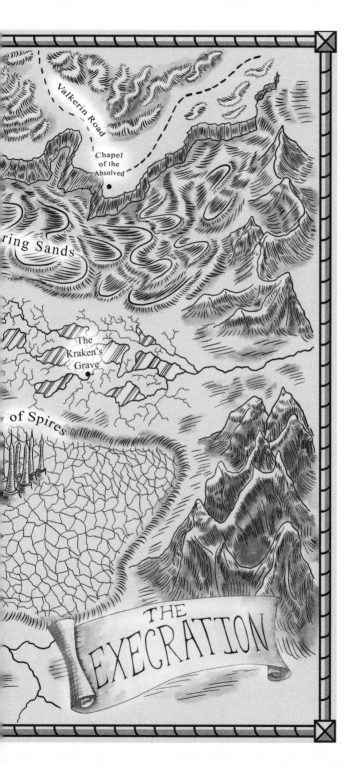

Put not thy faith in steel,
For flesh is always the stronger.
—*Injunctions of the First Risen.*

Chapter One

THE VALKERIN ROAD

•——◦——•

hy do you hate me so? Do we not do wondrous things together?
The questions were accompanied by a small pulse that coursed through the sword's handle into his palm, combining heat with an electric thrill that spread from his arm to the rest of his being in an instant. The sensation it provoked caused as much pain as it did delight and, no matter the countless times he had experienced it, had never become familiar.

A few yards away the raider spent his few remaining seconds staring at the tall man with the sword. The dying bandit swayed on his knees, one hand clutching the gaping wound in his throat whilst the other swished his scimitar about in automatic reflex. He seemed particularly transfixed by the tall man's sword, staring at the untarnished gleam of the blade, lacking the smallest speck of blood despite having just spilled so much of it onto the sands. The raider's horse, a fine wild-bred stallion, trotted back and forth in confused distress before coming to an abrupt, shivering halt as the tall man pointed the sword at it.

He loves his master, the voice observed as the tall man strode towards the animal, the sword handle pulsing again, this time with a sense of contrived compassion shot through with poorly concealed amusement. *Found him alongside the corpse of his mother when just a colt and raised him. Together they rode the fringes of the Execration for years and much booty did they garner from pilgrim and priest alike...*

"I have few thoughts to spare for bandits," the tall man cut in. "Regardless of how nice they may be to orphaned animals."

He jabbed the sword point into the raider's chest as he passed by. The pulse this time was full of the ravenous, raw need of something inhuman at feast. The raider's blood had completely faded into the steel by the time the tall man took hold of the horse's reins.

Hearing a scream from the direction of the caravan, he slid the sword into the scabbard on his back and mounted up. The stallion responded to his touch as if the man in the saddle had been riding him for years, spurring into a swift gallop. The caravan had been partially scattered by the raiders' initial charge, a dozen camels strung out along the verge of the old Valkerin-built road, either baying in alarm or nuzzling at the inert forms of slain owners. The tall man was surprised to see the corpses of several raiders amongst the fallen, some pierced by arrows, others evidently claimed by a blade, but one so gruesomely disarranged they were barely recognisable as human.

Ahhh, the voice said as the sword emitted a sense of pleased recognition. *There are other hungry souls here. Though, not so hungry as you, my liege...*

"Don't call me that!" the tall man snapped. It was by now an old admonition, one he knew the voice would continue to delight in ignoring.

He slowed the horse to guide it through the remnants of the caravan, passing plundered bundles that leaked silk, oils, spices and sundry other wealth onto the sands. There were more corpses here, but also some survivors. A portly man scrabbled about on the road's edge, gibbering barely comprehensible entreaties as he scraped coins from the dust. Further on a woman and child stared up at him from the shadow cast by the bulk of a slaughtered camel, eyes bright and unblinking in the gloom. A thin man with a ragged wound on his forehead stood guard on the pair, brandishing a long knife, the blade red down to the hilt. From the stricken but resolute expression on his lean features, the tall man divined him as being fully expectant of death. But still he stood, unwilling to abandon the woman and child.

Hearing the ring of steel on steel, the tall man spurred on, passing through a pall of displaced dust to draw up short at the ugly scene before him. The beast was about seven feet long from nose to tail, with long shaggy fur that covered its torso but left the legs bare. Raising a broad snouted head from the open chest cavity of a raider's corpse, it snarled, triangular jaws widening to emit a high-pitched yip of warning.

Oh my, the voice sighed in admiration as the hyena slunk away from the corpse, eyes still locked on the tall man. He recognised it as hailing from the crags near the northern coast, a far larger breed than its plains-dwelling cousins to the east, also notoriously vicious and intolerant of human company.

Aren't you lovely? the voice cooed, letting out a faint thrum of annoyance as the tall man reached over his shoulder to draw the sword clear of the scabbard. *Won't work,* the voice chided as he levelled the blade at the hyena, hoping to see the same shivering immobility it had wrought upon the horse. *She's too aware of the world, I'm afraid.*

The beast's eyes narrowed then, the snarl fading from its lips as it drew back, head shaking in confusion. *She senses me,* the voice noted with a delighted giggle. *Wonderful. I always wanted a pet.*

The hyena suddenly spun about as the sound of ringing steel pealed out once more. The tall man's gaze snapped to the sight of vague figures dancing in a haze of raised dust thirty paces on. His experienced eye knew this dance to be deadly, watching as one figure tumbled to the sand with a pained shout. The hyena immediately let out another yelp and surged into a loping sprint, closing the distance to the fallen figure in a few strides whereupon she clamped her jaws around the raider's skull. The crack of sundered bone was audible even above the tumult of clashing blades.

The tall man dug his heels into the stallion's flanks, sending him into a fast gallop. The dust thinned as he closed on the dance, revealing the sight of a woman whirling amidst a circle of five raiders. She lashed out continually with a scimitar as she spun, the triple braids of her hair trailing. He saw her score a hit on a bandit's over-extended arm, the scimitar biting deep and sending the man's tulwar to the sand. He reared back, cursing in the language of the plains tribes as he reached with his uninjured hand for a hatchet on his belt. The tall man's sword took his arm off at the shoulder as he galloped past then reined the stallion to a halt before bringing him about and charging once more. Only one raider made the mistake of trying to oppose him, his three surviving companions opting for the far wiser course of taking to their heels.

Yuk! the voice complained as the sword clove the unwise bandit's face in two. *A drunkard and a poppy fiend with a bad case of the pox to boot. Still,* it added as the blood faded into the steel. *A meal is a meal.*

The tall man watched the trio of raiders flee into the desert, pondering the notion of riding in pursuit. The sword's hunger, as ever, remained unabated, but he felt he had indulged sufficient distraction from his goal for one day.

"Chena!" the woman shouted. The hyena instantly rose from gorging itself on the raider's brains to sprint off in pursuit of the runners. The tall man watched them crest a dune and disappear from view, the hyena doing the same a few seconds later. The screams started soon after.

"Your help is appreciated, but was not required."

He lowered his gaze to see the woman retrieving a bow and an empty quiver from the sand. Her triple-braided hair had given him a clue to her origins, but the bow confirmed it. The weapon featured a composite stave of ash and buffalo horn affixed to a central grip formed of intricately carved black ivory. This was a beast charmer from the lands bordering the Second Sea.

Far from home, the voice noted, the tone laden with weary irony. *What could possibly have brought her here, I wonder?*

She looked up at him with a gaze of careful appraisal. He put her age at somewhere past thirty, but it was hard to gauge precisely under the black and white paint that adorned her features. He had some familiarity with the meanings of the myriad facial markings used by her people. The white circle in the centre of her forehead indicated a bereavement, whilst the three black dots beneath her left eye spoke of a purpose as yet unfilled.

A feud to settle? the voice pondered. *More likely a prayer she intends to make at the conclusion of a long and perilous journey. Don't you agree, my liege?* He felt the small pulse of pleasure in response to his anger as he returned the sword to its scabbard, choosing to ignore its additional taunt. *You know you should kill her. Only one prayer will be answered, after all.*

"You have a name?" the woman asked, frowning in bemusement at his continued silence. When he gave no answer she shrugged, shouldering her quiver. "I am…"

"Pilgrims do not share names," he interrupted, climbing down from the horse to inspect the still-twitching body of the one-armed raider. Like the others he wore a black scarf about his head, his body clad in a patchwork of armour and mail that bespoke a murderous career pursued across many lands. Pulling away the scarf revealed weathered features bronzed by the sun, though not so dark as those born to this region. Also, a silver chain dangling from one ear bore a small medallion of familiar design.

"The Church of the Arisen," the woman observed, peering over the tall man's shoulder at the silver teardrop. "Probably an old crusader left behind when the fanatics took to their ships. Many opted for the bandit's life rather than starve in the desert since no soul within two thousand miles would give them succour."

The tall man shifted the corpse to reveal the raider's belt and the swollen purse it held. Pulling it open, he spilled a clutch of coins into his hand. They were silver and newly minted, one side showing the head of a man he knew to be the current

Primate of the Church of the Arisen, the other bearing the same teardrop motif the raider wore at his ear.

"Seems someone succoured him," the tall man muttered, returning the coins to the purse and hanging it from his own belt. "You can have the plunder from these others," he added, climbing back onto the horse.

"How generous," the woman said, inclining her head. Her tone held a faint note of mockery that made him pause. Turning in the saddle to regard her once more he saw how her eyes lingered on the sword handle jutting above his shoulder.

"An unusual weapon for this region," she observed. "Not often you see a straight edge of such length. From the northlands, is it not? Just like this one," her boot nudged the raider's dead face, "and the coin he carried."

He said nothing, trying to close his mind against the voice's amused advice. *Kill her,* it told him in a sing-song chuckle. *She sees far too much. No one will know. Just another victim of these murderous villains.*

The woman's eyes narrowed as he continued to stare at her in silence, memories of far worse deeds crowding his mind. *Yes, my liege,* the voice hissed in hungry anticipation. *A small but necessary thing. And you have done so many necessary things…*

"Quiet!" he grunted, tearing his gaze from the woman.

"I merely asked a question," she said, the mocking tone more pronounced now. Did she think him mad? This grizzled, bearded stranger with a northland sword? If so, it didn't appear to provoke any fear in her which, in turn, stirred a small swell of appreciation in him. It was hard to remember a time he hadn't been feared.

A long, plaintive cry drew his attention back to the ruin of the caravan. People were emerging from the disordered chaos to weep over murdered companions and tend to the wounded.

Oh, how tedious, the voice complained. *This is always the worst part. Mewling mortals are so nauseating. Ride on. The chapel is only a few miles away.*

He guided the horse towards the nearest injured soul, a veteran caravaner with a gashed thigh being inexpertly tended to by a boy no more than twelve years old. "Too tight," the tall man told him, dismounting to pull away the bandage the lad had fixed on the older man's leg. "The wound is not so deep. A tight binding will starve the limb of blood and cause corruption…"

In all, some eighteen souls from the caravan had fallen in the attack along with twelve raiders before the remainder fled into the desert. The outlaws were stripped of all gear and valuables, some subjected to vengeful mutilation, and left to rot by the side of the road. By contrast, the dead caravaners were bound in coarse cloth and prayed over by their kin until dusk. As the sun dipped below the horizon they were borne to the top of the tallest dune and left to be consumed by sand and scavenger.

"The desert demands its due," the veteran caravaner with the injured leg said as the survivors moved on under the light of the half moon. He rode on the back of his sole remaining camel, his grandson plodding alongside under the weight of a pack laden with salvaged goods. The tall man had offered to carry the burden but the caravaner wouldn't hear of it. "Whether it's just the sweat of an untroubled trek, or the blood of those called to join their spirit to the wind, there's no such thing as a journey with no toll. Best the boy learns that now rather than later."

By mutual if unspoken agreement, the tall man and the woman kept apart for the remainder of the journey, he scouting the route ahead whilst she guarded the rear. Her hyena could be seen prowling the flanks throughout the two days it took to reach the chapel belonging to the Church of the Absolved.

It proved to be a building of unremarkable size or architecture, a yellow brick rectangle and conical tower perched on the edge of the escarpment overlooking the wasteland known to most as the Execration and to the priests who dwelt here as Alnachim, the Kingdom of the Absolved. He could see minimal signs of habitation, just a few tents pitched in the northward lee of the building and a solitary red-robed priest carrying water from the well to the chapel.

"We never linger here," the old caravaner said, eyeing the chapel with long-held suspicion. "Even the wind blowing from the Execration is said to carry a curse. The Allied Princes maintain a garrison at the oasis twelve miles on. We'll rest there." He watched the tall man climb down from the horse, hefting the pack that contained his few belongings. "You could come with us," he added, his voice holding more hope than expectation. "Always work for a keen blade and a strong arm on the Valkerin Road."

"I have business here." The tall man beckoned the boy closer and placed the stallion's reins in his hand. It was well known that horses would invariably go mad if forced to traverse the Execration. "He's yours now."

"You'll spoil the little bugger," the caravaner said, though not without gratitude.

"Change your bandage twice a day and soak the wound in garlic and lime juice," the tall man told him. He spared them a nod of farewell and turned to go, pausing when the boy spoke up, the first words the tall man had heard him speak.

"Don't do it." He spoke in a clipped murmur, casting a fearful glance at the tall man's face before turning a yet more fearful one toward what lay beyond the chapel. "They say the Mad God can't abide a kindly soul."

The voice's laughter was loud as the tall man laid a hand upon the boy's shoulder, looking into his earnest, fear-filled face and seeing so many others. *That day River Fork Keep fell,* the voice recalled with keen enthusiasm. *The Duke had three sons, if memory serves. The youngest was about the same age as this little shit. You should take his ear for reminding you. Just one, of course.*

"Then," the tall man said, taking hold of the boy and lifting him onto the stallion's back, "he will abide me quite well."

He watched the caravan trace its way east, keeping to the road as it skirted the escarpment for a mile before veering north. When it faded from sight he walked to the edge of the escarpment, looking down at the sheer cliff below before raising his gaze to the dark grey expanse that stretched away south for many miles. He could make out the hazy outline of mountains beyond the flat wasteland, painted red by the fading sun.

"They call it the Whispering Sands."

The woman stood a few paces off, her hyena at her side as she stared out at the grey waste. "But it's not sand," she went on. "It's ash. They say a mighty forest once stood here, all turned to cinders at the whim of the Mad God, and this was the least of his crimes."

"They say he also created everything south of these cliffs," the tall man replied. "Including the mighty forest. Is it a crime for a god to destroy what he made?"

"Perhaps not. But to destroy all those who lived under his protection certainly is."

"It might be best not to say so." He turned and started towards the chapel. "Should you have chance to meet him."

"I will." The hard certainty in her voice made him pause, turning back to see her daubed features set in a mask of implacable resolve. "Your actions in coming to the aid of those people speak well of you," she continued. "But know that I will have my prayer heard by the Mad God, whatever the price to my soul, my body or to any other who walks at my side."

It's a long way down, the voice pointed out, the tall man feeling the sword give a small tug towards the cliff edge. *A clumsy stumble by an ignorant barbarian. Who would question it?*

"Why would you imagine," he began, meeting her gaze, "that I am any less intent on my prayer than you are on yours?"

Because she thinks you're a hero, the voice laughed as the woman set her jaw, saying nothing. *She wants to spare you. How wonderfully naive. Still, she might at least let you rut with her before this is over. That's something, eh, my liege?*

He clamped his mouth shut to cage the rebuke, forcing himself to turn about and start towards the chapel. "Others have already gathered," he told the woman over his shoulder, gesturing to the tents pitched alongside the chapel. "With any luck we shouldn't have to wait very long. I suggest you sing your Sky Song now. I doubt the priests will tolerate it in their holy place."

Chapter Two

THE
WHISPERING SANDS

•)———(•)———(•

The priest was young, his features delicate almost to the point of femininity. To the tall man's eyes his recently shaven head and stooped posture made him appear diminished, cowed somehow, as did the tension in his neck and jaw.

Pain, the voice observed, something it never failed to recognise in others. *This boy has had a whipping in recent days. Not assiduous enough in his grovelling perhaps?*

"You require names," the priest said to those assembled in the chapel. There was no seating of any kind so they were forced to stand. The priest stood before the altar, a plain table of aged wood adorned only with a stone carving of a crescent; the symbol of the Absolved. The other priests, ten in all, were arrayed behind the altar, faces concealed within the cowls of their red robes. There were numerous discoloured rectangular patches on the walls, outlines of icons and tapestries that had hung here for many years.

Once the Church of the Absolved possessed many treasures, the voice explained. *All long since sold off to preserve this pathetic remnant.*

"Those who journey into Alnachim bearing their true name face swift damnation," the priest went on. "It is known. During our sacred trial you will know me only as Priest. I will answer to no other name. Now you must tell me what name you will answer to."

He turned an expectant gaze on the tall man, perhaps because he stood closest to the altar. *No,* the voice chided impatiently, *he senses authority in you, my liege.*

"Pilgrim," the tall man said. "Know me as Pilgrim."

Priest nodded and turned to the beast charmer. "And you?"

Her paint-covered brows creased in momentary consideration before she said, "Seeker."

Priest shifted his his gaze to the stocky man to her left. He was of pale complexion and clad in well-worn garb that spoke of a long journey. He bore no blades and carried a plain oak staff as tall as his head. "You may call me Book," he said with an affable grin. His words were spoken in Lenta, the most common tongue in the Alliance Lands, but coloured by a clear Northlands accent.

Standing to the rear of the man named Book was a taller figure clad in much finer clothes. He carried a heavy windlass crossbow on his back and twin daggers at his belt. However, his most distinguishing feature was the ornately engraved silver and brass mask that covered his face. Pilgrim thought it said much of the man's skill with weapons that he had traversed the Valkerin Road without being murdered for the mask alone.

"Player," he said with a florid bow. His words were spoken in a near-musical tone that complemented the floral engravings of his mask. Pilgrim had little difficulty in placing his origins;

Atheria, the City of Songs on the northern shore of the Third Sea, where those of noble status wore masks when forced to commune with the lower orders.

Standing several paces removed from the others were a man and a woman with the complexion of those born to the lands south of the Fourth Sea. The woman was strikingly handsome of face, with high cheekbones and an aquiline nose, clad in fine garb at odds with the more rough-hewn travelling clothes of her male companion. He was of less pleasing aspect, his features hardened near to the point of brutality. The scars Pilgrim noted on his forehead and jawline, together with his straight-backed bearing and the well-worn scimitar at his belt, marked him as a soldier of many years service. He would have taken them for high-caste mistress and mercenary bodyguard but for the marriage bracelets they wore. Looking closer, Pilgrim saw that the woman's beauty was not flawless. There was a certain redness to her eyes and shadows beneath her fine cheeks that might be due to the depredations of their journey across the desert, but he doubted it.

"You may call me Maisha," the woman said with a slight bow.

"Kusiph," the man said without opting to mirror his wife's gesture.

"Maisha and Kusiph?" Book asked with a bemused smirk. "The fabled lovers of Valkerin lore? Forgive me, friends, but I am sure you could think of something more original…"

"I am Maisha," the woman repeated in the same tone.

"Kusiph," the man said, although his voice now possessed a very slight edge and he fixed the northlander with a steady glare.

"Maisha and Kusiph it is." Book sighed, shaking his head and turning back to the altar.

"It is my sacred charge to set before you the hard truths of this pilgrimage," Priest informed them, his manner now one of studied gravity that made Pilgrim wonder how many times he had practiced this sermon. "You seek to stand before the Absolved and have him hear your prayer. To do that you must first traverse his kingdom, a place known the world over to be cursed. Where once there was beauty, now there is defilement. Where once there was life, now there is death. We the Servants of the Absolved have taken upon ourselves the holy duty of leading these pilgrimages. We do not do this so that you, the unbeliever, can seek favours from a god you do not worship, we do this so that he may hear our words, forgive our transgressions and restore Alnachim to glory.

"I will be your guide to the Crescent where the Absolved now dwells, you will be my protectors. Should you survive, your reward for conveying me to the Crescent will be a single prayer. If he chooses to answer, the Absolved will answer only one. This is known. In the two centuries since Alnachim fell into the state unbelievers now call the Execration, only three pilgrimages have reached the Crescent and only three souls survived to tell of it. The dangers are many, the way is long and it is likely we will all perish. Mark this well and spend this night in thought, for once the first step is taken on the Whispering Sands, there will be no turning back."

Priest paused, the tendons in his neck standing out as he straightened to look at each of them in turn, grimacing in pain but eyes unwavering. "Some of you may be given to selfish calculation," he went on. "You may be thinking, 'Since the Absolved will grant but one prayer, would it not be best if I were the only one to voice it?' Know that this is folly. The fewer of us, the more likely our pilgrimage will end before it ever catches sight of the

Crescent. And even if your prayer is heard, the Absolved may choose not to answer, for his ways are fickle now."

Fickle? the voice chuckled in scorn. *He's fucking mad and they know it. This clutch of deluded grovellers should have died out decades ago.*

"Go now and rest," Priest concluded. "Think long on my words. Any who still wish to make the journey find me here at first light. If you do not, leave immediately and sully this holy place with your disbelief no longer."

"It smells a bit like burnt toast," Book opined, nose wrinkling as he surveyed the grey expanse of the Whispering Sands. "Don't you think?"

"No," Seeker replied, running a hand through Chena's fur. The hyena's ears were flat as she gazed at the windswept grey dunes, apparently uncomforted by her mistress's touch. "It smells of death."

They stood at the foot of a narrow stepped track that descended in a zig-zag course from the chapel to the base of the escarpment. They had all appeared at the chapel come the dawn, none having found sufficient cause in Priest's words to abandon their purpose. Pilgrim couldn't decide if this made them a company of the brave or the mad.

Both, the voice chimed in. *I've always tended to think they're the same thing in any case.*

The Priest was the first to step onto the sands, immediately sinking to his knees as he did so, hands clasped and head lowered as the heavy cloak he wore whipped in the stiff wind. He spoke in a low murmur, the language unknown to Pilgrim and his companions, save Book. The stocky northlander's brows creased in an obvious sign of understanding as Priest's prayer continued. From his expression, Pilgrim doubted he found much comfort in the cleric's words.

Falling silent, Priest unclasped his hands and swept one over his head in a circular motion before getting to his feet. It was a gesture Pilgrim had seen many people make in the regions bordering the Execration, a warding against ill-luck or unseen danger, one that had evidently originated amongst the worshippers of the Absolved.

"Come," Priest said, starting forward. "We need to cover as many miles as possible before nightfall. The less time spent on the Sands the better."

He frowned when Pilgrim strode forward, taking up position at the head of their company. "You said you require our protection," he said when Priest seemed about to protest.

He turned about and started walking, eyes scanning the sea of monochrome dunes and finding it hard to credit that anything could subsist in such a landscape. There wasn't a scrap of greenery to be seen, nor any sign of water. But then, he knew enough of what these pilgrimages entailed to know the threat that dwelt here required no material sustenance.

Very true, my liege, the voice agreed, its tone for once free of any mockery. If anything, it was coloured by faint and rarely heard concern. *If you perish here,* it elaborated, sensing his surprise, *I might lie beneath this ash undiscovered for centuries. I respond poorly to boredom, as you know.*

They covered ten miles by noon, the loose ground making for slow progress. Although the sky remained mostly clear, the ashen plain seemed impervious to any pleasing aspect the sunlight might afford. It was, Pilgrim knew on an instinctive level, truly a place of death. There could no beauty in the Execration.

"Burning the great forest was in fact an act of salvation, you know," Book commented, sweat glistening on his balding pate and flakes of ash catching in his beard. Pilgrim had noted he seemed to find prolonged silence trying, or at least prolonged silence unbroken by his own voice. "The old Tributary Confederation sent a huge army to seize Alnachim who had few warriors to oppose them. And so the Absolved allowed them to cross his borders and, once within the confines of his cherished forest, he cracked the veil between the earth and the Infernus, letting loose the fires of damnation itself. Or do I misremember, my priestly friend?"

"You repeat an old blasphemy," Priest replied, though without apparent rancour. "The Absolved had no truck with the Infernus. This is a calumny spread by heretics to assuage the shame of their just defeat. The fires that consumed the forest were born solely from the Absolved's love for his people. He sacrificed one of the jewels of his realm to keep them safe."

"Quite so," Book acceded. "The chronicles make clear that many of the finest generals and warriors of the age met their end in the great conflagration. The Confederation collapsed into civil war shortly after, but the long decline of the Absolved's kingdom was also birthed in the fire that crafted this desert. It's been claimed that his descent into madness began here."

"You know much," Priest said in a neutral tone and Pilgrim found himself impressed by the youth's resistance to Book's scholarly taunts. "But, also very little. As you'll discover before this is over."

Pilgrim came to a halt when the sun reached its apogee but Priest insisted they press on without rest for as long as possible, drawing a complaint from Player. "Are we to suffer this trial without any refreshment?" he enquired in his melodious voice. The mask, of course, betrayed no expression, but Pilgrim somehow knew it concealed an eyebrow arched to an imperious angle. "Am I to slog across this desolation like some benighted churl?"

"Rest if you wish," Priest replied without pausing stride. "But do it alone, and know that you'll soon forget any notion of refreshment when you hear the first whisper."

Player came to a halt nevertheless, standing straight-backed and head raised in a pose that Pilgrim had seen on many a stage. It was termed 'the kingly stance', to be adopted by those favoured with a noble role, usually in one of the Valkerin Tragedies. "In my city," he began, "mere clerics know better than to command those of the Talented Caste…"

"Enough," Pilgrim said. The word was spoken softly but nonetheless silenced the Atherian. Pilgrim stared into the dark eye sockets of Player's mask, knowing the man behind it saw the dire promise in his own gaze. "Walk," he instructed.

Player's hand tightened on the strap of his crossbow, but whatever injured pride he might have suffered was evidently outweighed either by good sense or basic cowardice. Inclining his head, he resumed walking. Pilgrim allowed him to draw level before he too moved on. Showing his back to a man he had just humbled was never a sound idea.

The sun had begun to dip by the time Chena heard the first whisper, letting out a thin yowl of distress as she moved to Seeker's side. The company came to a halt as it reached human ears. It was little more than a murmur on the wind, lacking words, at least words they could comprehend, but unmistakably a voice.

Scanning the ash, Pilgrim saw nothing beyond displaced dust drifting across the dunes. None spoke as the whisper continued, rising in volume, the words still formless but now possessed of a questioning inflection.

"We may as well rest now," Priest said, sloughing off his pack. "Sleep as best you can before darkness."

"Wouldn't it be better to push on?" Book asked. "You said we should spend as little time here as possible."

"Until they find you." Priest undid the straps on his pack to extract a bedroll. "After that, it is simply a matter of enduring their attentions until daylight." Unfurling the bedroll on the ash he gathered his cloak around him and lay down. "You really should try to sleep," he added before closing his eyes.

The rest of them exchanged glances for a short time, the whisper and its question lingering in their ears. "I doubt I could sleep if I wanted to," Book said. "And shouldn't someone keep watch?"

"Only the dead persist here," Maisha said, the first words she or her husband had spoken since the trek began. "And their power is limited only to what you give them." She too opened her pack, extracting a flask which she sipped from before handing it to her husband. "A sleeping draught," she said. "Just one small sip will see you to slumber until morning, and deafen you to the voices of the dead."

Kusiph duly took a sip and handed the flask to Seeker who stared at it in reluctance before sighing and holding it out to Chena. The beast sniffed the flask and shrank back a little, but shuffled closer when Seeker stepped closer, extending the flask with insistent authority. Chena opened her mouth and Seeker allowed several drops of the draught to fall onto her tongue before taking a sip herself. Book proved less reluctant, holding the flask to his mouth for a decent sized swallow until Maisha snapped a warning and took it from him, handing it to Player. The Atherian turned away from them to lift his mask before drinking after which he fixed it firmly back in place and proffered the flask to Pilgrim. He glanced at it briefly before shaking his head.

"The whispers…" Maisha began.

"Let them come."

He unbuckled the sword from his back before spreading his cloak out on the ash and sitting down. He scanned the grey dunes and the drifting dust as the others lay down to let the draught take effect. Soon he was alone in his wakefulness, listening to the whisper grow louder as its question took on a terrible clarity: *"Who are you?"*

The sun was a red half-circle above the horizon now, drawing long shadows from the dunes that soon grew and coalesced as daylight faded. The whisper continued to ask its question as darkness fell. At first the unseen speaker seemed to be on his left, then an instant later, on his right.

"Who are you?" it asked again, closer now and directly to his front. The cloudless sky allowed the crescent moon to paint the sands in silver hues, every shadow seeming to creep towards him, although they froze when he focused on any one in particular. A sudden gust of wind stirred the ash and Pilgrim saw it linger on the outline of a figure. Before the breeze carried the ash away, he gained the impression of a large, bulky man in armour, wearing a horned helm and bearing an axe.

"Who are you?"

Pilgrim gave no reply, continuing to sit with the sword balanced on his knees, the voice indulging in a very rare silence. But he could still feel it even through the scabbard, the metal emitting an inconstant thrum he recognised as the closest the being that inhabited it came to fear.

"*Tell me,*" the whispering spectre said and Pilgrim felt it come closer, his breath misting as the air before his face chilled. "*What name do you bear? Why do you come here?*"

His skin prickled as the spectre began to circle him, his questions taking on a demanding, insistent cadence. "*Who are you? What name do you bear? Why do you come here?*" There was a pause and Pilgrim heard the thing hiss in frustration. Pilgrim felt tiny shards of ice scrape his skin as the spectre screamed, the sound filled with as much despair as rage. "*TELL ME!*"

He felt the spectre retreat when he gave no answer, its whisper becoming sorrowful. "*Once I was mighty. Once my name was known throughout the Five Seas. Bulvar the Axe, most feared of men. We came for glory, we found only flame…*"

The whisper ended abruptly as Priest let out a groan of distress, face twitching. The spectre's focus immediately switched to the cleric, a pall of dust rising as it swept towards him, repeating its questions with renewed urgency. "*Who are you? What name do you bear? Why do you come here?*"

Pilgrim saw Priest begin to writhe in his coverings, whimpering now as his features contorted. "*Tell me,*" the shade urged, a sheen of frost appearing on Priest's skin as it loomed closer. "*Tell me and I will join with you. Tell me and carry me forth from this place…*"

A sudden upsurge of whispers drew Pilgrim's gaze to the dunes where more dust was rising, the breeze outlining yet more figures, warriors all, shades drawn by the hunger of this long-forgotten axe wielder.

"Leave him be," Pilgrim said.

The spectre ignored him, Priest's face taking on a blue tinge as the air surrounding him grew ever more chill. His lips began to open, drawing back from his teeth in a reluctant grimace as he began to voice a word and Pilgrim had little doubt what it would be.

"Leave him!" He surged to his feet, the sword slipping free of the scabbard to slash at the spectre's vague shadow. It didn't try to evade him, apparently seeing little threat in mortal steel, and only realising its mistake as the blade's touch cut into its soul as easily as it did living flesh.

A blast of cold air whipped at Pilgrim as the shade of Bulvar the Axe screamed and recoiled. The babble of the others ceased instantly, as did their progress across the dunes. He heard only one voice raised, hushed and riven with terror. "*A demon-cursed blade.*"

"These people are under my protection," Pilgrim said, pointing the sword at the encircling shades as he revolved in a slow pirouette.

"*We wish only release!*" the axe wielder cried. The wind rose once more, revealing him again, now huddled and shrunken on his knees. However mighty he had been in life, he was pathetic in death. "*We came for glory and eternal misery is our only reward!*"

"You came for plunder," Pilgrim said. "You came for havoc. You came for rape. You came for slaughter. Your fate is deserved. Bleat at me no more." He levelled the blade at Bulvar. "Or feel the touch of this again."

When the spectre failed to flee he lunged at it, the sword scything through the dust left in its wake as it streaked away. Pilgrim turned the blade on the other shades, laying about as he moved across the ash, the sword moving with unnatural swiftness to shatter their circle and transform their whispers into shrieks. Soon he and his slumbering companions were alone on the sands.

I did not enjoy that, the voice informed him in a curt tone, sending a pulse of hot anger through the handle as he slid it back into the scabbard. *The taste of death cannot be savoured. Need I remind you...*

"You feed on the living," Pilgrim finished, resuming his seat on the ash. He flexed his fingers against the lingering sting of the demon's anger before returning his gaze to the dunes and their shadows. He could still feel them out there in the creeping shadows, but cowed by the sword and what lived within it. A once fearsome horde, now just a lingering stain on the site of their destruction. He felt they must have made for an impressive spectacle when they surged across the border intent on conquest.

You said they deserved their fate, the voice reminded him, sensing the pity swelling in his heart. *But then, you would know that best of all, would you not, my liege?*

He settled onto his side and slid into sleep to the sound of its mocking laughter.

Chapter Three

THE KRAKEN'S GRAVE

•)———(o)———(•

They cleared the Whispering Sands shortly after noon the next day. The ash dunes gave way first to a few miles of scrubland populated by stunted gorse bushes and tumbleweed, then to marshland that stretched away to east and west with no apparent end. A greyish mist lingered over the bogs and reed beds, Pilgrim noting the absence of any swarming bugs above the still waters.

"This was once the garden of Alnachim," Priest informed them as he traced a path to the east, eyes scanning the edge of the marsh. "Field after field of wheat and corn, fed by irrigation channels that carried water from canals dug to his design, water blessed by his own hand so that the crops grew tall regardless of the vagaries of the weather. No subject of the Absolved was ever hungry."

"Up until the moment he killed them," Seeker muttered. "It must've been a comfort to die with a full belly."

Priest confined his rebuke to a scowl before returning his gaze to the shoreline, eventually coming to a halt at a place where a road of shattered cobbles slipped from dry land into the marsh. Pilgrim saw his hands tremble before he confined them within the folds of his sleeves.

"No shades await us here," he told the company, speaking in a carefully measured voice, as if worried it might falter. "Here the danger is more...material in nature."

"Material?" Player enquired, Pilgrim once again sensing the raised eyebrow that accompanied the question.

"The Absolved loved the creatures of the earth as he loved its people," Priest said. "Gathering together a menagerie for his delight, and the joy of his subjects. When the kingdom fell they lingered, and were...changed."

"Changed how?" Book asked, now eyeing the misted bogs with deep suspicion.

"All beasts hunger, yet grow sated when fed. The beasts of the Absolved's menagerie know only hunger, regardless of how much they feed."

"It would help to know," Maisha said, breaking the heavy silence that followed, "what manner of beasts we will encounter."

"The Scripture of the Fall does not list them," Priest replied. "And much knowledge has been lost. We are left with but one phrase, 'And so did He gather together all manner of tooth and claw from every corner of the Five Seas.'"

"All manner of tooth and claw," Book repeated with a sour edge to his voice. "Wonderful."

"We're wasting time," Pilgrim said, starting towards the road. "Best prime that," he added to Player, nodding to his crossbow.

He took the lead with Priest close behind, the others strung out in single file with Seeker in the rear. She moved with her bow in hand and an arrow nocked to the string, Chena at her side, her maw quivering in a continual snarl as she stared at the passing marsh with baleful intensity. The mist concealed much of their surroundings and made navigation difficult. The old road they followed branched off in several places, the cobbles sometimes disappearing beneath the green-tinged waters for several yards. Whenever the route became obscure Priest would mutter which direction to take, Pilgrim finding it odd that he made no recourse to a map of any kind.

"All Priests of the Absolved are set to memorising the route to the Crescent from the moment they join the order," the cleric said when Pilgrim questioned his instruction to keep on through a foot-deep stretch of water. "Failure to recall it in its entirety is punished severely."

"Is that why you were beaten the day before we arrived?" Pilgrim asked.

Priest said nothing until they had sloshed their way through the obstacle, and when he did his answer was short, "No punishment is undeserved in service to the Absolved." His words had the cadence of an oft-repeated mantra that caused Pilgrim to conclude this would be a fruitless subject to pursue.

"They almost took you," he said instead. "Back on the Sands. Did you know that? You were about to tell a shade your name. Or did you think it just a bad dream?"

"I...would have warded it away. My faith in the Absolved..."

"Didn't protect you. And it won't. Shades don't care what you believe or how fiercely you believe it. Your name gives them purchase on your soul and thence your body. Next time, don't allow your arrogance to endanger this pilgrimage." He glanced over his shoulder, fixing Priest's gaze. "I am intent upon reaching the Crescent. Have no doubt I will do whatever is necessary to get there."

The youth stared back at him, fear and defiance plain in his gaze. He began to voice a reply but stopped at the sound of coughing from behind. Pilgrim retraced his steps to find Maisha sunken to her haunches, back bent as she let out a series of deep, wracking coughs. Kusiph crouched at her side, his hand massaging her back as he murmured comforting words.

"What is this?" Pilgrim asked, blinking in surprise as Maisha raised her head. Her features had undergone an abrupt transformation. The almost sculptural handsomeness was now a cadaverous mask of such deep-set illness he found himself resisting the urge to step back.

She's dying, the voice observed with its ever-keen eye for sickness. *Tumours are eating her lungs. She'll be lucky to last a month. At least now you know what she intends to pray for.*

"We need to stop for a time," Kusiph said.

"We can't," Priest insisted, casting wary eyes at the encroaching mist. "And all this noise will draw them to us."

"It'll take just a moment," Kusiph replied. He opened his wife's bulging pack and rummaged inside, emerging with a small green bottle. Removing the stopper, he held it to Maisha's lips.

"We…need to…preserve it…" she gasped, shaking her head before another bout of coughing wracked her.

"Please, beloved," Kusiph whispered, putting one arm around her shoulders as he pressed the bottle to her lips once more. This time she drank, her body convulsing as she swallowed, letting out a loud pain-filled moan.

The sound of disturbed water snapped Pilgrim's eyes to the left. It was just a faint splash, but it was the first he had heard since starting along the ruined road. The stretch of marsh visible through the mist remained as placid as ever, but the warning thrum from the sword told him they were being observed.

"We can't delay," he said, turning back to find Maisha climbing to her feet. As she straightened her hair parted and he saw that the cadaverous mask had disappeared, her features returned to well-crafted beauty, although he fancied there was more redness to her eyes now and the hollows of her cheeks more pronounced. Whatever concoction resided in the green bottle it evidently held remarkable restorative powers, albeit temporary.

Pilgrim began to tell Priest to point the way onwards, but then the sword let out a sharp trill of warning and his hand flashed to its handle. A loud splash sounded as he whirled, the sword guiding his arm and slicing with its preternatural swiftness, cleaving into the neck of the beast surging from the water. The blade cut through hard muscle and bone to sever the narrow-snouted, gape-jawed head from its shoulders. The huge scaled body it had been attached to writhed and twisted, long tail thrashing and four limbs twitching as black, foul-smelling blood jetted from the neck stump.

Disgusting, the voice complained, Pilgrim seeing how the dark viscous liquid slid off the blade's surface, rejected by the being within. *Animus ichor,* it added by way of explanation. *A potion from the depths of the Infernus. Evidently, the Mad God's pets died long ago, but this stuff animates their bodies and stokes the memory of hunger in what remains of their brains.*

"And yet they can still die," Pilgrim muttered in return, watching the crocodile's body subside into the marsh water, its death twitches fading.

Bleed them enough and they'll die, the voice confirmed. *But I doubt they'll all bleed so easily.*

Pilgrim straightened, turning to find them all regarding him with new eyes. The speed with which he had decapitated the crocodile spoke of something beyond human skill, stirring inevitable suspicion. As did his habit of speaking to someone none of them could see. Book seemed most troubled of all, his heavy, bushy brows drawn together in harsh and intent appraisal. It slipped away when Pilgrim met his eyes, the northlander forcing an affable but patently false smile as he inclined his head in appreciation.

"Quite an arm you have, friend," he said.

Beside him, Player suddenly raised his crossbow, aiming at a ripple in the water several yards off. "Save your bolts," Pilgrim told him. A swift survey of their surroundings confirmed the crocodile hadn't been alone, small dark protrusions broke the surface all around as eyes rose to regard their newfound prey.

"This way," Priest said, hurrying towards a fork in the road and taking the westward path. The rest of them followed in short order, matching the cleric's pace as he began to run. Pilgrim kept careful watch on the waters as they moved, seeing several scaled tails leaving broad wakes in the marsh water. As yet, none felt the urge to attack. What concerned him more was a swell he saw at the fringes of the mist. It moved in parallel to the reptiles but the height of the swell spoke of something far larger.

Player evidently saw it too for Pilgrim heard the snap of his crossbow's cord. The bolt birthed a white plume of water in the centre of the swell which failed to slow in response. Instead, it accelerated and began to sweep towards the road. Pilgrim saw long tails thrash the water as the crocodiles swiftly cleared a path for the larger creature.

"You fool!" Seeker cursed at Player. "You never provoke one of *them*, even were it not cursed."

"You know what that is?" Pilgrim asked her.

"I do. And we need to run faster."

A grunt sounded from up ahead as Pilgrim saw Priest make a short leap across a narrow gap in the road. He landed on firmer ground and immediately ran towards what appeared to be some form of ruin in the centre of a low islet. "Hurry!" he called over his shoulder. "It will shield us!"

Running in his wake, Pilgrim found little comfort in the cleric's claim as the ruins resolved out of the mist. Whatever this building was it had been big. A long series of curved pillars arced up to a height of over thirty feet, extending beyond the breadth of the island to descend into the marsh on the eastern side. There were gaps between each of the pillars, easily wide enough to allow entry of a man, and he doubted the columns were substantial enough to withstand a determined charge from the pursuing unseen giant.

"This is no fortress," he said, following Priest as he slipped between two pillars.

"No," the youth replied, staring at the structure's interior with both fear and wonder on his face. "No, it is not."

Pilgrim saw it then, the huge boulder lying in the centre of the long hall created by the two rows of pillars. He initially took it for a weathered sculpture of some kind, an abandoned statue to the Mad God. But, looking closer he saw no resemblance to any human figure. It appeared to be a large upturned font with stunted square wings extending from both sides. It was covered in moss which, when scraped away, revealed a dark, smooth surface very different from stone.

It's bone, my liege, the voice told him in the tone of a tutor to a dimwitted child. *Isn't it obvious where we are? What this is? Can't you feel it?*

Understanding dawned as Pilgrim's gaze tracked from the lump of bone to another several yards to his left, this one marginally smaller. A half dozen more lay beyond it, forming a line that disappeared into the marsh, leading to what appeared to be another islet. Like the bones, it was covered in thick green moss, but he could make out the dark recess of what was clearly an eye socket just above the waterline.

"Kraken," he murmured, eyes roving the huge skeleton that surrounded them. It had been a very long time since he had experienced a sensation of unalloyed wonder, but faced with the bones of so fabled a creature it was inescapable. Added to it was the sense of undeniable power lingering in these ancient bones. The voice was right; he could *feel* it like a hot wind blowing invisible sand against his skin. It was a far from comfortable sensation.

The thunder of hooves on firm ground tore his gaze from the bones to the sight of a huge grey bulk erupting from the water. The rest of the company had followed them into the confines of the kraken's skeleton, all staring at the beast as it charged towards the wall of ribs. It stood close to five feet tall at the shoulder with a bulbous body and stubby legs that nevertheless propelled its bulk at considerable speed. The most salient feature, however, was the huge vaguely equine head and gaping jaws, each corner of which featured a curved, straight-edged tooth. Whilst these were clearly not the teeth of a predator,

Pilgrim knew the force of the jaws' bite alone would be enough to crush the life from any man.

"What in the name of all the Risen is that?" Book asked, eyes wide with fearful bafflement.

"Water-horse," Seeker replied. She had her bow half-drawn and eyes locked on the animal as it drew ever closer. Next to her Player was frantically working the windlass of his crossbow. Pilgrim doubted either weapon would be capable of bringing down such a monster, even without the animus ichor flowing through its veins.

He hefted the sword as the water-horse came within a dozen yards of the ribs, but paused as it came to a sudden skidding halt. Letting out a loud huff the animal shook its head violently from side to side, taking a cautious step forward then retreating several feet with an alarmed grunt.

"The kraken was the most fearsome and powerful creature ever known to earth or sea," Priest said. "Even in death, all beasts retain the instinct to avoid it."

The water-horse gave off a low, rattling gurgle from deep within its throat as it began to pace back and forth beyond the ribs. It continued to stare at them all the while, eyes never blinking.

"Too scared to charge," Book observed. "But also too intent on our end to retreat. I don't give much for our chances should we venture beyond these bones."

Seeker's bow creaked as she slowly drew back the string, her gaze locked on the water-horse. It came to a halt as if sensing her attention, nostrils blowing twin gouts of steam as it matched her stare. Pilgrim was about to voice his doubts about the efficacy of assailing the beast with a single arrow, but stopped at the sight of Seeker's unblinking eyes and the unwavering steadiness of the arrow jutting beyond the bow stave. She continued to draw it until the fletching brushed her cheek, whereupon she let out a slow breath and loosed.

The arrow sank into the water-horse's eye for half its length, juddering with the force of the impact and surely scrambling what tissue lay beyond. The beast stood stock still for the space of three heartbeats, a rivulet of blood seeping from one nostril, then it collapsed, sinking down onto its belly and lying still.

Clever, the voice opined. *Even a body driven by the ichor needs a brain to work.*

"A remarkable feat, my lady," Player told Seeker with one of his florid bows. "Why, not even fabled Juseria herself could match such skill."

"Juseria?" she asked.

"A legendary figure from the Kraken Wars," Book explained. "Said to have been blessed with peerless bow skills by the Valkerin gods."

"Quite so," Player confirmed. "I was once honoured to play her murdered brother in The Barbarian's Feast. Even the harshest Atherian critics agreed it was the most accomplished and convincing poisoning ever to grace the stage."

"I seem to recall it as a minor part," Book said with a poorly concealed smirk. "Only six lines, I believe."

Player stiffened a little. "A master of his craft requires no lines to move an audience, sir. With six, I could move a world."

"Can you move those?" Seeker enquired, gesturing to the waters beyond the island. There were too many scaled heads bobbing above the surface to easily count. The reptiles lingered some thirty feet from the shore and showed no sign of coming closer, but also no sign of leaving. Even if she could sink every arrow in her quiver into an eye, there would still be an abundance of predators to greet them when they left the safety of the Kraken's grave.

The bone, my liege, the voice said. *The kraken's essence lingers in its bones, not the place.*

Pilgrim turned to the moss-covered vertebrae, running a hand over the dark surface he had exposed. It was hard material, and tingled to the touch, but he felt a faint sense of give in it, like old wood. Raising the sword, he waited for it to thrum then brought the blade down on the wing-like protrusion on the flank of the bone, severing it from the main body. Several more strokes, delivered with sufficient speed to make the blade seem a silver blur, resulted in seven evenly sized chunks.

"Here," he said, tossing a piece to each of his companions. "Keep them close."

"Are you sure?" Book asked, eyeing the lump of bone in his hand. "Will a mere fragment be enough to keep them at bay?"

"We'll find out shortly." Pilgrim raised a questioning glance to Priest who pointed to a northward stretch of road beyond the wall of ribs. "Unless you'd rather stay here and starve."

He stepped between the ribs without pause, striding along the aged cobbles to the island shore where it met a small, part-ruined bridge. The sound of displaced water drew his gaze to a quartet of reptiles peering at him from the marsh. He held the bone fragment up and advanced towards them, grunting in satisfaction as they all promptly disappeared below the surface.

"It appears we have procured ourselves safe passage," Book said, grinning in approval.

"There is no safe passage in the fallen kingdom," Priest said. He went to the tumbled bridge and began to make his way across. "There are other things here that even the Kraken would have feared."

Chapter Four

THE CITY OF SPIRES

•)———(•)———(•

The crocodiles continued to trail them through the marsh, multiple long wakes marring the still waters on both sides of the road. They would occasionally veer towards the shore only to scramble away in a welter of flailing limbs and tails when Pilgrim or one of the others brandished their shards of bone. Eventually, as the ground grew firmer and the waters more shallow, the reptiles disappeared. The Mad God's menagerie, however, was not done with them yet.

At first Pilgrim took them for some unfamiliar form of vegetation, dark, jagged shapes hanging from the bare branches of tall trees that now began to dominate the landscape. As they passed beneath, it became clear these trees bore a different kind of fruit. The first creature to unfurl its wings revealed a fox-like face and large pointed ears. The wings were easily the length of a man from tip to tip and the beast's body the size of a large dog. It twisted as it detached itself from the branch, letting out a chirp that was more of a scream, hurtling towards them with wings half furled and long fangs bared. They all raised their bone shards and the creature seemed to halt in mid-air as if it had struck an invisible roof. Hissing, it spread its wings wide, sweeping itself aloft. The other creatures all fell from their branches in unison, swooping down on the company before retreating to a safer height as they sensed the kraken's power.

"Flying jackals," Seeker said, one hand clutching her bone shard and the other her scimitar as she squinted up at the circling beasts. "Great bats from the southern jungles."

"We must press on," Priest insisted. "If we don't reach the city before nightfall..." He left the rest unsaid but it was clear to Pilgrim that this forest held more dangers than just flying jackals.

The cloud of bats continued to circle above as they made their way through the forest, joined by other colonies roused from the treetops by the scent of fresh prey. They maintained a safe distance for the next hour but grew progressively bolder as daylight began to wane. The company found itself repeatedly ducking as the bats swooped down in groups of two or three, each time descending lower than before. One proved unwise in its angle of approach, swooping just low enough for Chena to leap up and clamp her jaws on a wing tip. The bat's scream was brief, cut off almost instantly by the crack of breaking bone when the hyena crushed its ribcage. She cast the corpse away with a whine and retched at the foul taste of ichor.

The first spire came into view shortly after, resembling the blade of a giant poniard thrust up through the earth. The trees had fallen away now, leaving a landscape of cracked, dry soil. The flying jackals forsook their pursuit as the company reached the long shadow of the spire, stretching away across ground painted red by the fading sun. Pilgrim was learning that, in the Execration, true colour only came with the sunset.

He found himself coming to a halt at the sight of what lay beyond the spire. The city stretched away into a crimson haze, spire after spire, some linked by bridges and walkways, although most of these had fallen away. What remained resembled the spearpoints of a titanic host.

Rather reminds one of the commencement of the night march towards Saint Maree's Field, the voice recalled. *How many swords under your banner then, my liege? Forty thousand, wasn't it?* It paused to offer a sigh of wistful nostalgia. *Will we ever see those days again?*

"Quickly!" Priest urged, breaking Pilgrim's momentary fascination. He resumed his run, following the cleric as he led them towards a steep ramp at the base of the spire. "We have to get inside before dark."

Pilgrim was surprised to find a sturdily built door of oak and iron at the top of the ramp. The wood beams and metal bracings all seemed to lack the age and decay of the ancient stone that surrounded it. He was also relieved to find it unbarred and open. Priest had yet to explain the need to find shelter before nightfall, but from the near-frantic manner with which he pushed the door wide and gestured for them to get inside, Pilgrim felt little compunction in following him into the gloomy interior.

The door slammed shut the instant they all made their way into the building, leaving them in near-pitch darkness. Pilgrim heard the hard rattle and clatter of a heavy lock being turned as Priest secured the entrance.

"I don't suppose," Book said, "anyone thought to gather firewood?"

There was a rustle of leather and fabric as Maisha unbuckled her pack, followed by a faint liquid sloshing. The light that banished the darkness had a green tinge to it, revealing a broad circular space lacking anything save a dust-covered tile floor and a circular stone stairwell. It traced along the spire's wall, curving up into the darkness that waited above.

"Glow worm sap," Maisha explained, giving a wan smile as she shook the glass jar in her hand. The light emanating from it increased its glow a fraction, Pilgrim noting how it revealed yet deeper shadows beneath her eyes. Seeing his scrutiny she looked away, staggering a little and causing Kusiph to come to her side.

"She needs to rest," he said, glaring at Priest with an expression that dared him to voice a challenge.

"We all do," Priest agreed. "We can't venture out until daylight in any case."

"Why?" Seeker asked. "What's out there?"

"Over a million souls dwelt in this city before the fall. Many remained in its wake, and they are not quiet."

He glanced at the door as he spoke, causing Pilgrim to take a closer look. "This is no more than ten years old," he said, running a hand along the rust-free iron of the lock.

"Ours is not the first pilgrimage," Priest replied. "Not all were sent with the intent of reaching the Crescent, but to prepare the way for those that would."

"How long has it been?" Book enquired. "Since the last pilgrimage, I mean to say?"

"A year." The cleric's face clouded and he gathered his cloak about him, moving to sit down at the base of the staircase. "Eight souls led by our Arch-Prelate, the head of our order. Only one returned, a woman who came to pray for knowledge.

She had been a great scholar in her homeland, feted for her wisdom, but thirsted for more. How she made it back to us will forever be a mystery. When she walked out of the Whispering Sands her eyes were gone from her head, torn out by her own hands, and yet she was smiling. 'He answered my prayer,' was all she said and would offer no word on the fate of our Prelate. She refused all offers of help and wandered into the desert. We never saw her again."

None of them said anything to break the silence that followed, instead all finding what comfort they could and settling down for the night. They clustered close to the light from Maisha's jar, eating a sparse meal from the rations provided by the priests in the chapel. It was bland fare, consisting of hard tack and some form of cured meat which only Chena seemed to find appetising. After the meal, the jar's glow began to fade, regardless of how vigorously Maisha shook it.

"I have more," she said, voice weary as she reached for her pack.

"Best to save it," Pilgrim told her. "I'm sure many dark places await us."

He fell to slumber shortly after, as the last of the green-tinged light fluttered and died and one of his companions gave voice to a faint but fearful whimper. For himself, he slept soundly. The dark had never scared him.

He awoke to the sword's insistent thrum, accompanied by an irksome prodding from the voice. *Kindly rouse your royal arse, my liege! Something's here, and I greatly dislike its stink.*

For a second he saw only darkness but rapid blinking revealed a dim line of burgeoning light below the door. A quick survey of his companions found them all still asleep, save two.

"Seeker?" he whispered, the hiss of it echoing long through the empty interior. There was no answer from the beast charmer, nor any yelp from Chena. Pilgrim rose and went to the door, finding it still locked.

Look up, the voice told him. It held an uncharacteristic edge of impatience, leaving him in little doubt of the scale of the threat it sensed. His gaze tracked the winding spiral of the staircase into the shadows of the spire's lofty reaches, seeing nothing, but his ears did detect a very faint sound. "A child?" he wondered aloud as he gained an impression of a forlorn, sorrowful wail.

No, the voice stated. *It most definitely is not.*

He kicked Priest awake as he rushed to the foot of the staircase. "Trouble," he said, starting to scale the steps. "Wake the others."

Judging by the number of steps, his most conservative guess as to the height of this structure was somewhere close to a hundred and fifty feet. It made for a laborious ascent that birthed a plethora of aches throughout his body by the time the stairs levelled out. *Getting old, my liege,* the voice said, its urgency apparently insufficient reason to resist a jibe, one it had been making for several decades now. Pilgrim ignored it with accustomed ease and made for the tall arched opening in the wall. It led out onto a walkway of impressive breadth, but stunted length, having been tumbled to ruin some fifty paces from the archway. He could see Chena pacing back and forth, head moving from side to side in agitation, pausing frequently to nuzzle the side of her mistress who seemed not to notice.

Seeker knelt at the ragged edge of the walkway, arms out-stretched as she voiced whispered, tear-choked entreaties in her own language. Although he couldn't speak her tongue, Pilgrim detected several words it shared with the less obscure dialects from the southern shore of the Second Sea. "Please...I searched...my love..."

Careful, the voice cautioned as Pilgrim moved closer. *If a shade has learned her name...* The sword's thrum was like a throb now, but he resisted drawing it. Chena, he suspected, might not react well to so patent a threat.

"Seeker," he said, keeping his voice low. She gave no sign of having heard, continuing to utter her whispered pleading, her gaze locked on something in the void ahead. Pilgrim squinted as he drew near, at first seeing nothing but then making out a shape in the air. It was formed of various hues of grey but was not insubstantial like the shades that plagued the Whispering Sands. This was as solid as a living soul could be, a girl of perhaps ten years clad in rags that barely covered her skin. She stared at Seeker with her small face set in a frown of hard accusation. Also, Pilgrim saw as he looked closer, although she stood as if on firm ground, there was only air beneath her bare feet.

"Please..." Seeker said, arms moving in a beckoning gesture. The girl's frown deepened and she made no move to come closer.

"What is this thing?" Pilgrim asked the voice.

It paused before answering, its tone one of cautious bemusement. *Dream wraith. Our barbarian friend must have had a troubled sleep. Wraiths don't require names to snare their prey, just a wayward dream will do. I must say, my liege, I do wonder why you care so. It'll lure this one to her death and feast on her despair at the moment of expiry. One less prayer for the Mad God to choose from and you remain blameless in the eyes of our fellow pilgrims.*

"Please…" Seeker repeated, rising to her feet and shuffling towards the edge of the walkway, arms outstretched. "I'm sorry…"

"How do I vanquish it?" Pilgrim demanded, reaching to grip the sword's handle.

Not with me, it replied. *It has her on its lure now. Only she can break it. The Mad God must truly have hated his worshippers so, to unleash such horrors upon them.*

Watching Seeker's foot come within an inch of the edge, Pilgrim reached for her arm. "There is nothing…" he began, then reared back as she whirled, her scimitar hissing from its sheath.

"Don't touch me!" she snarled, lowering herself into a fighting crouch. "You will not keep me from her!" Chena let out a confused growl, shuffling closer to her mistress and whining in plaintive inquisition.

"There is nothing there!" Pilgrim jabbed a finger at the scowling little girl. "This is merely a phantom plucked from your memory."

"Liar!" She lunged, the scimitar slicing the air an inch from his head. "She is what I came for. The Absolved has already answered my prayer. My daughter is returned. You would stop me to ensure your own prayer is heard. It chooses only one."

"To pray you must stand before him at the Crescent." Pilgrim kept his tone one of calm insistence, hands raised and open. "You know this. And you know *that*," he jerked his head at the wraith, "is not your daughter."

She tore her gaze from his, turning back to the girl. It had changed now, its eyes taking on a red glow, perhaps an unwitting emanation from the being that wore it like a mask. Its accusatory stare, however, remained firmly in place. "It has to be," Seeker breathed. "I have searched for so long since the slavers stole her. Spilled so much blood. It can't all be for nothing."

Chena growled again, but this time there was no query in the sound. The hyena's lips quivered as she bared her teeth, claws scraping stone and the thick fur of her neck bristling like thorns. Where before she had seemed incapable of sensing the creature, now she glared at the phantom girl with feral enmity. Leg muscles bulged as she tensed, crouching in readiness for the leap, jaws snapping in anticipation.

"NO!"

Seeker launched herself at Chena, dropping her scimitar to wrap her arms about the hyena's neck. "No, dearest one."

So, the voice said as Seeker buried her head in Chena's fur and wept. *Love severs the lure, it seems.*

Pilgrim lifted his gaze in time to see the wraith's mask dissolve. The little girl twisted, head swelling and limbs elongating, the creature's solidity fading into something that resembled a smear of silver grey gossamer. He caught a glimpse of a gnashing, toothless mouth and glowing red eyes riven by a combination of misery and fury, then it was gone, whirling away between the spires just as the sun broke to paint them with a dull yellow glow.

Chapter Five

THE
LIBRARY OF BONES

◦)━━━(◦)━━━(◦

T he ground remained a uniform plain of cracked, hard-
packed soil as they made their way between the towering
spires. Over the course of several miles throughout the next
day, Pilgrim saw no vestige of the roads, walls or parks he
would have expected to find in such a huge conurbation.

"It's a sea bed," Book explained. "Except the sea has long
since vanished. Boiled away by the Mad God's rage, was it
not, my priestly friend?"

"The spires rose from the waves of the Azure Sea, it is true,"
Priest replied, his unperturbed tone once again displaying a
resistance to the scholar's caustic observations. "But the sea
didn't boil, it drained when the dams to the west collapsed."

He spoke with a slightly distracted air, his gaze moving
constantly between the passing spires, often lingering on the
various doors and windows. Like the spire they had sheltered
in the night before, each featured a ramp that ascended to a
flat platform surrounding the tower's base. Pilgrim assumed
these must have been used as jetties, logical architecture for

a city that rested atop water. He found the scale of the place remarkable, dwarfing all of the cities he had visited save eternal Valkeris, and even the vast temples and titanic statuary of that fabled testament to human ingenuity were said to be a denuded shadow of its former majesty. But Valkeris possessed a layered authenticity to it, the maze of streets bespoke a place that sprawled and changed with the ages. This place possessed a sense of falsity, more a monument than a city.

He built it because he could, was the voice's opinion. *The vain ambition of a god succumbing to madness, perhaps? Or, mayhap he just thought it would look pretty.*

Although the day's journey proved to be the least hazardous so far, Priest insisted on setting a punishing pace, permitting only the briefest rest. Maisha had evidently partaken of her curative for she managed to keep up for much of the day until early evening when her energy began to fade along with the sunlight.

"It's not much further," Priest said when Kusiph demanded they call a halt. The cleric's eyes were darting about continually now, flicking from one spire entrance to another with bright-eyed scrutiny.

"Something lurks within the spires," Pilgrim said. "Waiting for darkness. What is it?"

"As I said," Priest replied. "Many perished in the fall, many remained. Please," he added, turning back to Maisha, "we cannot tarry here."

She nodded wearily and removed the stopper from her bottle. As she raised it to her lips Pilgrim judged its contents to have shrunk to perhaps one third of what it had been back on the Sands. *She won't make it,* the Voice said. *The tumours will claim her long before she even catches sight of the Crescent. It would be kinder to leave her here with her man, let them perish together in peace rather than face the trials ahead.*

Pilgrim detected no cruelty in the voice, just objective reasoning that he found hard to argue against. Nevertheless, he joined Kusiph in helping Maisha to her feet once the curative had taken hold.

"Strange to find a good man on such a mission," she told him with a grateful smile as they resumed their rapid march.

"Yes," Pilgrim agreed, turning away. "It would be."

They pressed on for another hour until the now-familiar red glow began to paint the westward flanks of the spires. By then the largest structure yet had begun to loom up from the cracked earth a mile ahead. It was unique in being formed of three spires, the tallest yet seen, linked by a sheer wall. As they drew nearer and the light grew ever fainter, Pilgrim detected a low but steadily building murmur to their rear. A backward glance revealed nothing, but a thrum from the sword confirmed the imminence of danger.

"Ignore it," Priest instructed. "Keep going."

The murmur grew louder as they ascended the ramp to the three-spired building and Pilgrim realised a portion of the noise was coming from within the structure, specifically the tall arched opening in its base. Instead of going inside, Priest led them past the arch to one of the spires. Looking into the gloomy interior beyond the entrance, Pilgrim's eyes detected a faint impression of movement. At that moment the noise grew louder; he had little doubt it was in response to their presence. It had a hungry, desperate note to it that was unmistakably human and he deduced it was in fact an accumulation of voices, a good many voices.

"I have to climb," Priest said, coming to a halt at the foot of the spire. Although it was weathered and uneven in many places, Pilgrim saw little prospect of scaling it.

"How?" he said. "There are no handholds."

"There is a route," Priest muttered, eyes narrowing as they tracked up the wall to a narrow opening some fifty feet above. "I just need to recall it." He stepped up to the wall and reached for a small indentation, hauling himself up then reaching for another. "Wait here," he said, continuing to climb. "There's a rope ladder secreted aloft."

He moved with a steady fluency, his hands finding purchase on holds Pilgrim's eyes had failed to detect. All the while the murmur grew louder and the sunlight fainter.

It occurs to me, my liege, the voice commented. *This cleric may have no need of us from this point hence.*

Pilgrim concentrated on the route the priest took, trying to commit the location of the various handholds to memory. However, his efforts were interrupted by a sudden snarling growl from Chena and a sharp thrum from the sword.

The hyena had sunk into her customary crouch that indicated an imminent lunge. Seeker stood at her side, bow drawn and arrow pointed at the archway. Her gaze lacked the usual focus, instead her expression was one of alarmed bafflement. "What in all Five Seas is that?" she wondered in a horrified whisper.

At first Pilgrim took the shapes extruding from the archway as the emergence of some many-tentacled beast, another monstrosity from the Mad God's menagerie. But then he saw that each appendage featured a hand, the long-nailed fingers clenching repeatedly like the claws of a hawk. They would occasionally jerk back into the recess of the arch whenever they caught the merest flicker of sunlight, but as the seconds ticked by they did so with markedly less frequency and more and more emerged to claw at the air. Pilgrim looked up to gauge Priest's progress, seeing the cleric reach the narrow opening and begin to haul himself inside.

An upsurge in murmuring drew his attention back to the arch. As the sunlight dimmed to a faint glow a head emerged amongst the mass of clawing hands. Pilgrim thought it might once have been a woman, but it was hard to tell. The face was desiccated, the skin ragged and fallen away in places to reveal bare bone. Tendrils of black hair hung down from a denuded scalp to frame a face riven with boundless hunger, the jaws opening and closing to clamp together what few teeth remained. The eyes were the only feature that could be described as alive, the pupils shrunk to mere dots in greying orbs that neverthe-less shone with a vibrant hate.

Dritch-wight, the voice said. *It appears the Mad God didn't just curse his pets.*

The creature pulled itself free of the wall of flailing arms, Pilgrim seeing that it wore threadbare rags that did nothing to cover the flaccid dugs of its breasts and distended sex. He wondered if his disgust showed on his face for the wight became enraged then, its hungry groan abruptly shifting to a shriek. It lunged towards him with a speed he wouldn't have thought its stick-like limbs could produce, the clawed talons of its hands reaching for his throat.

The hard snap of a crossbow's lock sounded and a bolt appeared in the wight's forehead. It tottered for the space of a heartbeat, the hate fading from eyes that rolled back in their sockets before the thing collapsed into a bundle of rags and withered flesh. Black ichor leaked from its forehead and mouth, the stench of it causing them all to move back several paces.

"You can thank me later, sir," Player told Pilgrim, raising his crossbow as he inclined his head.

Pilgrim said nothing, drawing the sword as another creature stumbled clear of the arch, swiftly followed by two more. Unlike the woman, they evidently felt no need to pause before launching themselves at the living intruders, each shrieking as they charged, taloned hands outstretched. Seeker's arrow took one, the shaft spearing it through the head, whilst Pilgrim sliced another in two with a lateral slash of the sword. Kusiph tackled the third, darting forward to stab the point of his scimitar into its chest with professional accurary. The thing failed to die, however, countering with a slash of its claws that Kusiph only just managed to duck under. The wight lunged for him again, then shrieked even louder when Pilgrim brought the sword down on its outstretched arms, severing both at the elbow.

"The heart won't do," he informed Kusiph, whirling to lop the creature's head from its shoulders. Ichor erupted from the stump in a black geyser as it slipped to the ground, twitched and lay still. The upper half of the wight Pilgrim had cut in two continued to crawl towards them, nails digging into the stone as it dragged itself on until Player stepped forward and stamped a boot onto its head, crushing the skull.

Stronger than he looks, the Voice observed. *There's more to this one than just a mask and a good deal of pretension.*

"Back!" Pilgrim said as more wights emerged from the arch. They swarmed towards them in a thick mass a dozen strong, closing the distance quickly only to be cut down. The sword scythed through three with one stroke, whilst Seeker's arrows and Kusiph's scimitar did similarly deadly work. As he swung the sword, Pilgrim cast repeated glances up at the opening, the voice's warning of Priest's possible treachery gaining more resonance with every second he failed to reappear.

And I thought the reptiles tasted foul, the voice griped as Pilgrim cut down the last wight, a spindly wretch no more than four feet tall that might once have been an adolescent, whether boy or girl he couldn't tell.

"Is that all of them?" Book enquired. He stood backed up against the spire wall, eyes wide with terror and his staff clutched in his hands. Pilgrim couldn't see any stains on the staff.

"It seems so," Kusiph said, cautiously stepping forward to peer into the arch. "Looks empty."

"This is but one spire, remember," Seeker said. She stood staring back the way they had come, Chena at her side, snout blackened and retching as she cleared the ichor from her throat. Beyond them Pilgrim saw a mass of small dark figures emerging from the base of every spire in view. Although rendered ant-like by the distance, he could discern their shared direction. He had learned long ago how to swiftly estimate the strength of an approaching army and put the number of creatures now shambling towards them at well over ten thousand, and growing. *Many perished in the fall, many remained.*

"Priest!" he called up to the opening in the wall, putting all the authority he could gather into the summons.

For several long seconds there was no response then the cleric's youthful face appeared in the opening. "Apologies!" he called. "Some fool decided to hide it!"

The rope ladder clattered down the wall an instant later, and Book lost no time in scrambling up. Maisha went next, moving with all the agility she could muster, though from the way her shoulders sagged when she reached the top, the effort had clearly cost her.

"After you, sir," Player told her husband with a courteous bow. "I would never dream of separating Maisha and Kusiph. It's my favourite tragedy."

Kusiph nodded his thanks and quickly followed his wife up the ladder. Player turned to Pilgrim, his mask tilted at a questioning angle. "Consider this my thanks," Pilgrim said, gesturing for him to go ahead.

As the Atherian scaled the wall, Pilgrim watched the approaching horde. Their number had swollen to what must have been over thirty thousand and the first were only moments from the ramp. Their shambling gait altered as they neared their prey, taking on a predatory speed.

"Go," Pilgrim told Seeker, pointing to the ladder.

"You first," she said. "Chena can't climb that thing and I'll need your arm to haul us both up."

There was no time to argue the point so he rushed to the ladder and swiftly scrambled to the top. Seeker ran to grab one of the wooden struts whilst Chena clamped her jaws about another. The ravenous former denizens of the city crested the top of the ramp as Pilgrim, Kusiph and Player hauled the ladder up the wall. The weight of both Seeker and the hyena was not slight and both Priest and Book were obliged to add their strength to the effort. Clawed hands missed the beast's dangling paws by inches as the pair were drawn clear.

"By the Risen," Book gasped, groaning in relief as mistress and beast finally reached the opening. The horde's combined cries rose to a feverish pitch as they both clambered inside.

Pilgrim looked down to see them thronging the base of the structure in ever greater numbers, every face upturned, jaws gnashing and eyes filled with a uniform hate.

"Piteous devils," Kusiph said, features bunched in mingled sorrow and disdain as he surveyed the wretched mass. "Do you think they remember? Possess some knowledge of who they were?"

Of course they do, the voice said with an amused snort. *The ichor works differently on a human body. Dritch-wights remember but remain slaves to their hunger and hate. I find I admire the inventiveness of the Mad God's punishments more and more.*

"Just mindless beasts," Pilgrim said, turning away. "What they were matters not."

Maisha lit another of her glowing jars as night fully descended, the green light revealing a huge interior. The centre of the level they stood on lacked a floor, creating a black triangular void surrounded by platforms of numerous storeys ascending into darkened heights. This level was lined with numerous shelves from floor to ceiling, all laden with thick mounds of dust. He heard Book let out a soft groan of despair, watching his shoulders slump as he swept detritus from one of the shelves.

"Gone," he hissed in an angry mutter. "All gone."

"What is this place?" Pilgrim asked Priest.

"The Great Library of the Absolved." The cleric moved to one of the shelves, dabbing his fingers to the dust. "Said to contain the wisdom of all the world. He sent emissaries to every land to buy books, recruited scholars to write yet more. For three centuries this was the greatest centre of learning known to humanity, surpassing even the colleges of eternal Valkeris." He grimaced, working his fingers to banish the dust. "Now vanished forever at the order of the Absolved. As he cursed his people, so he cursed his books."

He turned to the others. "Best eat and garner what sleep you can. After tomorrow, it's likely to be a rare comfort."

The company made their way deeper into the building to find a resting place, keen to get away from the unending hungry chorus of the horde. The wights had invaded the base of the spires, the cries echoing up through the building with aggravating clarity, but Priest assured the company the stairwells between the spires and the library proper had been destroyed long ago. They settled on a mostly bare expanse of floor dotted with the remnants of chairs and tables that Priest asserted must have been a workplace for the library's scribes. Pilgrim crafted a small fire from fragmented sticks of furniture which proved dry and easily lit. Sleep came quickly for the others save for him and Book.

The northlander fashioned a torch from a rag tied about a chair leg and set off to explore the building on his own, proving deaf to Pilgrim's advice that his time would be better spent at slumber. He left him to roam the empty floors and sat tossing sticks into the fire to keep it lit. He knew sleep would not claim him tonight. It had often been the way, even in the days before the sword and the voice, the aftermath of battle left him restless.

Not restless, the voice corrected. *Just wanting more, like a drunkard who can't sleep for thinking of the one more goblet of wine he could have had. Except one was never enough, was it, my liege?*

"Thank you for banishing any doubts I may have had about this enterprise," Pilgrim replied, drawing a soft chuckle in response.

You really think the Mad God will answer your prayer? You, amongst these others? I doubt Book and Player offer much competition, but a dying woman with a devoted husband? A mother in search of a stolen child?

"He will or he won't. If he doesn't, rest assured I'll find another way."

A muffled shout came from above, accompanied by a flicker of light from Book's torch that silhouetted a rotted rail before moving swiftly on.

Perhaps he's found something to eat him, the voice suggested. *If so, why disturb its meal?*

Pilgrim rose and retrieved Maisha's glowing jar which she had left close to the fire. Its luminescence had diminished to a faint gleam but, once shaken, provided enough light to guide his way. Luckily, the builders of this place had chosen to craft their stairs from stone rather than wood, allowing for an easy ascent. He climbed several floors before once again catching the flicker of Book's torch. This level differed from the others in lacking a triangular hole in its centre. Instead it was formed of connected chambers of various dimensions, each one featuring a long rotted cot and desk. They were arranged in a circle around the large central chamber where he found Book on his knees amidst what Pilgrim soon identified as a substantial pile of human bones.

Book started at the sound of Pilgrim's footfalls, rising and hefting his staff. He faced Pilgrim with an expression of determined, if fearful resolution, his stance that of a man defending a treasure hoard rather than a cluster of old bones.

"This doesn't concern you," he said, forcing the words from a dry throat. "These are mine."

Pilgrim ignored him and moved towards the bones. He saw Book tense as if preparing to bar his way, but wisely thought better of it. "I have silver," he said instead, fumbling for his purse. "Leave me be and I'll…"

"Be quiet," Pilgrim told him, squinting in surprise as he plucked a thigh bone from the pile. The light from Maisha's jar played over the surface to reveal some form of script etched into the bone. The lettering was tiny, but still executed with considerable skill and precision.

"You're wasting your time," Book said. "The language is ancient, lost to the ages…"

"It's Ultrean," Pilgrim said, squinting yet further as he read on. "'Know well that thy faith is not birthed unbidden in thy soul, but grown as a cherished tree so that, in the fullness of time, its fruit may blossom and so bless the world.'" He switched his gaze to Book, seeing sweat now covering his brow. "One of the Injunctions of the First Risen, if I'm not mistaken."

He tossed the bone back onto the pile and reached for a skull. The text covered it from upper jaw to nape, Pilgrim picking out a passage from the Dialectics of the Third Risen. He set it down and reached for a vertebrae, finding a collection of quotes from Saint Agnet, founder of the first outposts of the Risen Church in the northlands. And so it went, every scrap of bone he examined had been etched with scripture, all of it from the same church. A church he knew all too well.

"I can tell you see the value in this," Book said, speaking in a cautious but earnest whisper. "Your accent may have faded over the years and the sun has burnished your skin, but I know a man of the north when I see one." He reached out with a tremulous hand to clutch at Pilgrim's sleeve. "Your church requires your service."

"So," Pilgrim said. "I see there is more than one priest on this pilgrimage." He jerked his head at the bones. "Is this what you came for?"

"In part. So much was lost in the Ravager's wars. His persecution left vast tracts of scripture in ashes. In the hundred years since we have done much to recover what was lost. Learned priests like me were sent to gather what we could from foreign lands. Long has it been a legend of our faith that the Church of the Arisen had a presence in the Kingdom of the Absolved. Now," he cast a reverential glance at the bones, "it is proven beyond doubt. These," the tremble in his hand increased as he withdrew it from Pilgrim's sleeve, extending it over the pile, "may well contain the most complete repository of scripture in the known world."

"And you have no questions as to how it came to be here? Church scripture was originally set down in Valkerin, yet these are all inscribed in Ultrean, a language that died out at least a millennia before the advent of the church. And I doubt any human hand or instrument could set letters into bone with such precision."

"A mystery to be answered," Book insisted, "when we reach the Crescent."

"That is what you intend to pray for? Knowledge?"

"I intend to pray for something that should have happened when this kingdom fell. I will pray for the Mad God's death."

Pilgrim sighed in derision. "You expect him to just will himself into extinction? Mad or not, I find that hard to credit."

"Something happened here." Book's expression became fierce as he leaned closer, his voice an urgent whisper. "Something vile, unnatural. Something that fractured the holy concord between the earth, the Higher Realms and the Infernus. It is my belief the nascent church tried to stop it, and failed. I will complete their mission. The truth of the Risen Word cannot be denied. When the Mad God hears it, he will have no choice but to yield."

Staring into this fanatic's glaring eyes, Pilgrim felt an old but familiar need building in his breast. It required no stoking or taunts from the voice. This was all his own. How many like this had he killed? Most quickly in the fury of battle, some slow in the aftermath, and none of it regretted. He couldn't remember the full number, but faced with this one, just as unreasoned and implacable as all those others, he felt it hadn't been too many.

"On the journey to the chapel of the Absolved," he said, voice soft, "I happened across a caravan under attack from raiders. On one of their bodies, I found this." His hand went to the purse on his belt, extracting one of the coins stamped with the sigil of the Risen Church. "You said you had silver."

Book blinked, his fervour fading as he shuffled back. "I hired men to escort me across the desert," he said. "What they did afterwards was their own affair."

He's lying, my liege, the voice drawled as if smothering a yawn. *Just snap his neck and have done. Or take your leisure over it as was your wont when time allowed, I seem to recall. I doubt our fellow pilgrims will miss him much.*

"Hired men?" Pilgrim asked. "Former crusaders gone renegade but still loyal to the church would be my guess, especially when paid. Did you send them after the beast charmer, or were they simply ordered to slaughter any caravan they found?" The slight tic in Book's gaze told him he had found the target. "Trying to improve your odds, then," he added with a smile. "For a man so certain of his mission, you seem keen to ensure only your prayer is heard at the Crescent."

Book's eyes flicked to the doorway and back again, fresh sweat beading his skin. However, Pilgrim could see his resolution remained despite his fear. It had often been the way with true adherents, those few who never allowed their terror to unseat their faith no matter how many fingernails he plucked, eyes he gouged, or hot irons he pressed to their flesh. But then, none faced the test that awaited this one.

"I'm not going to kill you," he told Book. "In fact, I'll do everything I can to ensure you reach the Crescent, for I suspect I will find the Mad God's answer to your prayer highly entertaining."

Chapter Six

THE
CRUCIBLE BRIDGE

◦)━━━(◦)━━━(◦

In the morning, with the dritch-wights vanished from the dry bed of the Azure sea, Priest unfurled the rope ladder and they clambered back down. He left the ladder where it was, causing Maisha to ask, "Is that wise? The wights may use it to get inside."

"It matters not," was the cleric's only response, striding down the ramp without delay.

"But, other pilgrims..." she began, but fell silent when Pilgrim moved to her side, speaking quietly.

"There will be no other pilgrimages," he said. "We're the last. Or, at least the last who will be guided by the Church of the Absolved. I suspect others will come as long as the Mad God lingers."

Once again, Priest set a rapid pace and they drew clear of the spires by noon. The cracked earth continued for several miles, broken by what at first appeared to be outcrops of jagged rock that resolved into the wrecks of ancient vessels as they drew nearer. Most were small, fishing smacks and barges, but one was immense. It formed a hundred-foot-long elongated oval upon the earth, the planks of its hull bleached to a pale grey and the iron of its nails and fittings rusted red. The only intact feature was the figurehead at the prow, an elegant carving of a young man with flowing hair and outstretched arms. Priest came to a halt in its shadow, sinking to his knees with hands clasped.

"Is that...him?" Seeker wondered, peering up at the wooden statue as Priest murmured his prayers. The figure's features were cracked and partially misshapen by the elements, but the beauty of the youth's face remained somehow intact. His finely muscled chest featured a symbol rendered in Ultrean lettering, though the word was unfamiliar to Pilgrim, but not apparently to Book.

"It's Thandril," he said, his tone dull. He stood at a good remove from Pilgrim and had kept to the rear of the company throughout the day, face set in a permanently wary scowl. It seemed he expected his true mission to be revealed at any moment and rightly feared his companions' reaction. From the new bulge in his pack, he had apparently selected but one skull from the pile of inscribed bones in the library. Pilgrim spent scant energy pondering which had been chosen amongst so many, as it seemed unlikely the man would ever bear it beyond the Execration.

"Who?" Seeker asked.

"The human consort of the Absolved," Book explained. "Said to be the most perfect man ever to grace the earth. The Absolved was smitten at the first glance they shared, as too was Thandril. It's said their love endured for more than a century, the youth kept youthful by the Absolved's devotion. But all love fades, as does all beauty."

"Was he cursed like everything else here?" Seeker reached up to run an appreciative hand over the statue's wooden thigh. "It would seem a terrible waste."

"The legends say he grew tired of life," Book said. "He remained young whilst his family and friends withered and died, an old man trapped in a prison of youth. The Absolved showered him with riches and comforts, built palaces and, as this wreck attests, great pleasure barges to soothe his troubled heart. But it was never enough. Finally, Thandril prayed to his divine lover for release and, though it pained him, the Absolved granted his prayer. All the depredations of age came upon Thandril in an instant, and he died."

"Is that what did it?" Maisha wondered. "Did the heartbreak drive the Absolved to madness?"

"No," Priest stated, unclasping his hands and getting to his feet. "The Absolved grieved for his lover and decreed he be honoured for all the ages to come, but his grief did not descend into madness. For the next two centuries, his love for his people sustained him."

"But all love fades," Book said, offering a bland smile in response to the cleric's sharp glance.

"The Crucible Bridge lies five miles west," he said, striding off. "To reach the Crescent, we need to be across it before dusk."

The great dams that had once held back the Azure Sea rose like a long row of stunted teeth against the perennially overcast sky. As they drew nearer, the sound of rushing water became ever louder, eventually swelling to a continuous roar.

The source became clear when Priest led them up the broad steps to the Crucible Bridge and the deep gorge between the ruined wall of dams and the irregular granite massif opposite stood revealed. A raging torrent of roiling water rushed through the gorge, birthing a perpetual mist as it rebounded from the enclosing rock.

Pilgrim estimated the length of the bridge spanning the gorge at perhaps a third of a mile. It was narrow for much of its length but opened out into a circle twenty paces across at its half-way point. In the centre of the circle a large statue of an armoured warrior stood atop a rectangular plinth. The warrior wore armour of archaic design, echoing ancient depictions of Valkerin legionaries with its overlapping plates and broad-based helm covering the head from crown to neck. It stood with its gauntleted hands resting on the pommel of a huge tulwar, the black, empty eye-holes of its helm staring east in unmoving vigilance.

Priest paused before setting foot on the bridge, turning to them with grave, almost apologetic sincerity. "Here we come to the point where no guidance from me can help you," he said, shouting to be heard above the torrent's roar. "The Crucible Bridge was constructed to guard the path to the Crescent. Famously, Alnachim had no warriors, the Absolved being determined to spare his people the horrors of war. And so, in need of a guard, he made a warrior of iron and filled it with his will, giving unto it the power to discern the thoughts and intentions of others. All who pass over this bridge must endure the warrior's scrutiny. Put no faith in your capacity for deceit. Take no succour from what lies you have told others or yourself. The warrior will see it all, and in seeing he will change you, for to know unalloyed truth is to be changed. That is why the Absolved named him the Crucible."

He turned back to the bridge, straightening his back as he gathered his resolve. "Proceed only if you are willing to be judged," he told them before starting forward. "And know that the Crucible's judgement is merciless."

I suppose it would be fruitless to state, the voice said as Pilgrim followed Priest onto the bridge, *that I consider this a very unwise course of action.*

"I do not fear judgement," Pilgrim murmured, his words swallowed by the raging spate below.

I can sense what resides within that thing, the voice persisted. *And it isn't judgement. It's a lock on a door that will permit no inhuman passage. And I, as you know, am very far from human.*

The sword began to thrum with increasing energy the closer they drew to the Crucible. Pilgrim soon realised his first sight of it had misled him as to the statue's size, thinking it approximately man-sized. In fact it stood at least twice the height of the tallest man. The metal from which it had been fashioned was weathered but lacked any sign of rust, despite the many years spent in proximity to the constant pall of vapour from beneath. Although it remained utterly still as they came within the scope of its shadow, the sense of scrutiny was strong, birthing a certainty that more than just a void lurked behind the empty and impassive eye-slits of the warrior's helm.

However, it wasn't until they came within a few paces of the plinth that Pilgrim began to feel it, a hard, prodding sensation behind his eyes. It wasn't painful at first, but the sense of intrusion that accompanied it roused an instinctive aggression. He found himself trying to shield his mind, force out the intruder with visions of unyielding walls or endless seas. It shattered them with laughable ease and, for the first time in many years, Pilgrim knew panic as his memories were laid bare.

"No!" he grunted, eyes closed tight and hands clamping to the sides of his skull. "No. I don't want to see!"

He was dimly aware of stumbling, his shoulder colliding with the plinth as his feet lost purchase on the bridge. The cries and exclamations of his companions reached his ears, but it was all far away, lost in the tumult of memory that consumed him. Fire, battle and blood flitted through his mind, glimpsed briefly but with terrible clarity. Every death, every torment suffered and inflicted, every plea ignored and every cruelty indulged. One image lingered longer than the others, this one bloodless, but also the worst. A young woman with long, honey-coloured hair that fell to her waist, smiling as she whirled in girlish glee amidst a field of poppies. The petals rose in her wake, scattered like rubies into a clear sky.

"Loise!" he heard himself voice her name, one he never spoke aloud, the word emerging as a strangled cry from a cage of clenched teeth. The memory of her death was a waking torment, but the memory of her alive and joyous at that first meeting lashed at him, cut him worse than any blade.

Perhaps it was the sense of being cut that caused the intruder to move on, fix upon the image of the sword, lying bright and untarnished amidst the dusty forgotten archive in which he had found it. The memory of the first thrum of the handle in his grip when he claimed it, the dark exhilaration of knowing that with this all the vengeance he craved would be his.

The intruder recoiled then, the vision of the sword first trembling then shattering as a sense of recognition filled him, a single word shouted into his mind, made furious with enraged repugnance: DEMON!

The world returned in a rush, leaving him on all fours, gasping for air as his heart hammered against his chest like a trapped animal desperate for release. For a second, the pounding of his pulse was all he could hear, but then came a squeal of grinding metal followed by the familiar whoosh of a blade. Many years of battle-born instinct saved him, forcing his limbs to propel him into a roll. Sparks showered him as the tulwar's tip scraped along the tiles of the bridge's surface. He saw Player dodge the upsweep of the blade, the edge catching a glancing blow on his mask and sending him into an overhead tumble. He landed on the marble parapet with the kind of force Pilgrim knew would lacerate organs with the shards of shattered ribs.

Hearing the tulwar cut the air once again he tore his gaze from the Atherian's immobile form and darted forward, drawing the sword as he did so. He was obliged to leap in order to ensure the blades met, the collision of unnaturally forged steel producing a blinding flash of released energy and sending Pilgrim careening across the bridge. He collided with a marble buttress only a few feet from Player's body, still lying across the balustrade, his masked head hanging in the air. Pilgrim's surprise at seeing no blood seeping from the mask was short lived, as the sound of metal feet on stone drew his gaze back to the plinth to see the Crucible leaping down. Its body squealed with every movement as it rose from its crouch and turned to confront him. The helm's eye-slits were no longer empty, filled instead with a bright yellow glow, as full of hate as any dritch-wight's.

I told you it wouldn't like me, the voice reminded him as the iron warrior started forward. Pilgrim drew in a ragged breath and tried to force himself to his feet, only managing to rise to one knee by the time the Crucible's shadow fell upon him. It loomed above, tulwar raised, then paused as one of Seeker's arrows rebounded from the back of its helm. A faint hiss issued from the depths of the warrior as it turned, either an expression of irritation or some result of the workings of its divinely crafted body.

Pilgrim saw Seeker moving to the Crucible's right, hands blurring as she loosed shaft after shaft at the metal giant. It let out a faint, tinny grunt as one of her arrows found an eye socket, sinking in all the way to the fletching. However, unlike the water-horse in the marsh, the hoped-for demise failed to materialise. Instead the Crucible raised a gauntleted hand to pluck the arrow free, sparing the barb a brief glance before flicking it away and turning back to Pilgrim.

He had regained his feet now, and much of his wind, enabling a swift sideways roll as the tulwar came flashing down. Marble tiles cracked and parted like paper, producing a fountain of dust and shattered stone. The tulwar's edge sank deep into the bridge's surface, sticking for the brief moment it took the Crucible to tug it free. Seeing his chance, Pilgrim rushed forward and leapt, raising the sword high and bringing it down with all the strength he could add to its demonic force. It glowed as it descended on the warrior's metal wrist, severing hand from arm.

The Crucible emitted a groan as it straightened to regard its missing hand. Smoke rose from the glowing edge of the stump but this man of metal seemed to feel no pain, exhibiting only a vague curiosity as it angled its head. The yellow glow of its eyes flickered before it lowered its damaged arm and stooped, reaching with the other for the tulwar's handle.

Pilgrim made another charge, sweeping the sword in a horizontal arc at the Crucible's right leg, but this time his opponent was swift in spotting the move. His handless arm jerked back, catching Pilgrim on the shoulder and batting him away with all the ease of a man swatting a bothersome bug. He somersaulted, landing hard a dozen feet from the plinth. The force of the impact should have jarred the sword loose from his grip, but, of course, that could never happen.

The Crucible straightened, tulwar in hand, and began to turn, then froze as one of Maisha's jars shattered on its back. The pale yellow liquid within the jar changed the instant it splashed across the warrior's metal skin, taking on an angry red glow and birthing a thick veil of grey smoke. The Crucible arched its back as the substance ate into its armour, a note of pain clear in the groan escaping its helm. Gaping holes appeared in its back, gobbets of blackened metal sloughing away as it staggered. Pilgrim had a glimpse of the warrior's inner workings before it reeled about, seeing a mass of whirling gears and levers lit by a yellow glow surely beyond the comprehension of a mortal mind.

The Crucible swayed like a drunkard near the end of his revels, wreathed in smoke and jerking spasmodically as Maisha's concoction reached its innards. But life still remained in its eyes, their glow flaring bright as they fixed upon the source of its distress. Something akin to a snarl emerged from the helm as it lurched towards her, the tulwar sweeping down then up with a blurring swiftness.

Maisha stared at the approaching warrior in frozen terror until Kusiph barrelled into her side, pushing her clear an instant before the tulwar's edge slashed across his chest. The blow possessed sufficient force to lift him off his feet and propel him over the bridge's edge, leaving an arc of blood to mark his passage into the torrent below.

Maisha's scream was a wordless, searing thing as she rushed to the balustrade, frantic arms outstretched as if she could somehow summon her husband from the depths. Her speed was such that she came close to toppling over before Seeker caught her about the waist, bearing her down as she thrashed, her scream of grief choking into hard, desolate sobs.

An ugly clicking drew Pilgrim's gaze back to the Crucible, finding the metal man now on its knees, jerking as the gears within him disintegrated. It performed a parody of a human retch, tiny shards of metal erupting from the helm in a cloud of sparkled smoke. Then, with a very tired final groan, the warrior collapsed onto the bridge's surface. The glow of its eyes flared, fluttered and died, leaving it a smoking, lifeless ruin.

A cough came from beyond the column of smoke and Player staggered into view. His mask was slightly askew and he took a moment to straighten it before surveying the scene in evident shock. "What in the name of the Endless Song happened?" he asked, and Pilgrim heard not the slightest vestige of pain in his voice.

Not so great an actor after all, the voice observed in a caustic drawl.

Chapter Seven

THE
SUPPLICANTS' PATH

•)———(•)———(•

*I*t's the mask, the voice said. Its tone held a note of reflective self-admonishment Pilgrim hadn't heard before. He found it odd and more than a little disconcerting. Whatever the myriad faults of the being that lived with the sword, its sense of certainty had at least provided a measure of surety if not comfort throughout their many years of mutual bondage. *Some kind of glamour on the mask. That's why I didn't see it.*

They had left the bridge behind an hour before, entering the huge arched portal at the point where it met the granite massif. Maisha had initially refused to move, speaking in a monotone whisper, her eyes empty of anything save grief. Seeker eventually coaxed her to her feet, though the combined depredations of her loss and illness meant Pilgrim had to assist in conveying her into the tunnel. Their way was lit by an iron torch with dry coals in its basket found sitting in a stanchion at the tunnel mouth, presumably another gift from servants of the Church who had sacrificed themselves to prepare the way. At Pilgrim's insistence, Maisha had partaken of her curative at their first rest stop a mile or so into the feature-less passage. She drank it all in one gulp and tossed the bottle aside before sinking down into a huddle, knees drawn up and face buried in her crossed arms.

With its attention fixed on Player, the voice felt no need to offer dark witticisms on Maisha's grief or observe that the loss of her husband might mean she no longer felt any desire to pray to the Mad God. These conclusions Pilgrim reached by himself, though they shamed him. Her intervention had saved his life, and he retained an attachment to the notion of an unpaid debt.

He won't be easy to kill, my liege, the voice said, its concern expressed in a sharp thrum from the sword. Pilgrim glanced over at Player, sitting nearby and rubbing his ribs as he sighed in apparent distress. *It would help if I knew his rank. I'd guess Fourth Circle...*

Pilgrim closed his mind as it droned on, as it was given to do when obsession took hold. Once it had chattered on for three solid weeks without interruption regarding the need to kill an outlaw band on the western coast of the Fifth Sea, the result of some ancient vendetta birthed long before Pilgrim had ever grasped the sword's handle. In the end he had hunted down and killed every miscreant over the course of two months just to shut it up. In the aftermath, he began to take a keener interest in tales of the Execration and the Mad God who answered the prayers of those willing to risk its countless dangers.

"I assume this tunnel has a name?" he asked Priest who sat close by. "Everything in this place seems to."

The young cleric seemed distracted, his eyes set in the con-centrated stare of one subsumed in memory. "The Supplicants'

Path," he said after a short interval. "The route followed by those who survived the Crucible's scrutiny."

"May we assume," Player said, the empty ovals of his mask tracking over the bare brick of the tunnel wall, "it will not be as uninteresting as this for its entire length?"

"Only the true devotee of the Absolved may walk the Path to the Crescent." Priest got to his feet, face still set with the same distracted concentration. "We've rested long enough," he said, hefting the torch and starting off down the passage.

To Pilgrim's relief, Maisha didn't need further coaxing to follow along, although she did so in vacant-eyed silence, apparently deaf to all questions. It took an hour of walking before a glimmer of silver light appeared in the tunnel ahead and another hour before it opened out into a cavernous chamber. It stretched away for several miles, every yard of it seemingly filled with arched pillars supporting walkways and steps that tracked in different directions. Some rose to great heights whilst others seemed to disappear into the dark bowels of the earth. The whole spectacle was lit by some form of luminescence in the cavern roof that resembled a scattering of stars and provided sufficient light to make their torch redundant.

Priest showed the same regard for the item as he had for the rope ladder in the City of Spires, tossing it into the void below the platform upon which they stood. Pilgrim took it as another signal that this was the last pilgrimage his church would lead. Priest turned to the right and started down a stairwell, the base of which formed a junction of five separate walkways leading off into the stone forest of pillars.

"Which one?" Player asked.

Priest said nothing, moving from one walkway to another, eyes lowered and brow creased. Following his gaze, Pilgrim saw that the start of each path featured a carved inscription. Like the inscribed bones in the library, the letters were rendered in Ultrean. However, whereas Pilgrim had little trouble deciphering the Risen scripture, these words made scant sense. Names he couldn't pronounce featured amongst references to constellations and places of which he knew nothing. It appeared to him as little more than gibberish, but to Priest it evidently meant a great deal.

"This way," he said, starting along a path that led into what appeared the densest part of this angular stone maze. As he followed along with the others, Pilgrim glanced down at the words engraved into the stone. It was as meaningless to him as the others apart from a symbol he had seen carved into the wooden flesh of the figurehead on the dry bed of the Azure Sea.

"Thandril," he muttered.

They proceeded to traverse a bewildering succession of walkways and stairwells, Priest pausing at every junction to read the inscriptions set into the dark granite. In each case, Pilgrim recognised Thandril's symbol but nothing else. After close on two hours of following the cleric's course, it appeared to him they had made meagre progress across the cavern. It was almost impossible to be certain amongst all the overlapping construction but he was sure they had passed by the same spot several times. Priest, however, continued to trace their route without any particular sign of hesitation or confusion. He proved as deaf to questions as Maisha and ignored all suggestions they might rest. It was only when they came to the top of the tallest stairwell they had yet ascended that Seeker's insistent but softly spoken command brought them to a halt.

"Stop."

Pilgrim turned to find her crouched at Chena's side. The hyena's thorny hackles were raised as she dipped a twitching nose at a mark at the edge of the stairwell's summit. It was far too irregular to be another inscription, a six-inch-long scar in the stone that resembled a honeycomb in the way whatever had created it had eaten into the granite. Although it appeared bare of any substance, Chena let out an angry yip as she sniffed the mark, retreating several paces, lips quivering in a snarl.

"What is it?" Pilgrim asked Seeker.

Seeker didn't reply immediately, instead unslinging her bow and nocking an arrow, her gaze shifting from the mark to the confusion of hard-edged shadows below. "Something's here," she said.

"Wights?" Book said with a barely suppressed quaver to his voice.

"No." She angled her head as the pitch of Chena's growls increased. "Something...else, and it has our scent."

"We must move on," Priest stated, his tone emphatic and none felt inclined to argue.

They descended a steep procession of stairs to a long walkway, the terminus of which disappeared into a confluence of shadows. Some corners of this place were beyond reach of the star-like substance in the cavern roof. Maisha took one of her glow jars from her pack and shook it as they entered the shadows, the green radiance banishing the gloom but also revealing a dozen or more honeycomb marks on the stone.

"Do you know what could do that?" Pilgrim asked her.

"Acid," she replied. "Or some other form of caustic." She spoke with a tired resignation, her face taking on the cadaverous aspect indicating the curative was fading from her veins. He expected her to stumble to a halt at any moment, but somehow she contrived to keep pace with the company despite the bouts of coughing that began to wrack her.

"'From out of darkness hope shall arise,'" Player recited when they exited the shadows, a line from an Arethian Resurgence-era comedy the name of which Pilgrim couldn't remember. The walkway came to a halt only a few yards on in a T-shaped junction, one path leading right, the other left. Once again, Ultrean symbols had been carved at the start of both.

"A moment," Priest said, moving to examine the inscriptions.

"This is not a good place to loiter," Seeker said. She still had an arrow nocked to her bow and her eyes roved constantly over the surrounding patchwork of light and shade.

"Just..." Priest waved a hand, his brows knitted in consternation as he moved from one symbol to another. "Just one moment."

Feeling the sword start to thrum Pilgrim watched him pace back and forth twice more before moving to his side. "What's the delay?"

"Thandril," Priest said, pointing to the now-familiar symbol set into the inscription on the right. "Also," he pointed to the carving on the left, "Thandril. All the surviving scripture is clear, to achieve the Crescent, one must follow Thandril's path. He being the first supplicant, the first to have his prayer answered by the Absolved."

"It could mean both paths are valid," Book suggested, moving closer but staying clear of Pilgrim's reach.

"No." Priest shook his head. "No. Only one will take us to the Crescent."

"We can't stay here!" Seeker stated loudly as Chena let out a warning growl. Both stood facing the confluence of shadows they had emerged from moments before, the beast charmer's bow half drawn.

Book gave an exasperated sigh and hurried to inspect both inscriptions. "An even more archaic form of Ultrean than I'm familiar with," he mused, running unsteady fingers through his beard. "With Lysian influences if I'm not mistaken."

"Is this relevant?" Pilgrim snapped. The sword's thrum was constant now, accompanied by an impatient tuneless hum from the voice.

"They aren't identical." Book pointed at the left-hand inscription. "The translation may be rough, but I believe it says 'Lo Thandril, stride towards thine eternal love.' Whilst this one," his finger jabbed to the right, "reads 'Thandril, dost thou not know to crawl in thine contrition?'"

"Stop jabbering and choose!" Seeker grated, eyes still locked on the shadows. Following her gaze, Pilgrim saw no sign of movement, nor any sound that might indicate another presence. Nevertheless, the sword left no doubts regarding her judgement.

"It has to mean something," Priest said. "Choose the wrong path and we could wander here for days."

"We won't have days," Seeker said. "Nor do we have minutes."

"Is it not obvious?" Player said. He turned to address the Priest with one hand on his hip as he casually gestured with the other. "Supplication. This is the Supplicants' Path. A supplicant would crawl, would he not?"

Book and Priest exchanged a glance, the young cleric sighing in relief. "My thanks, sir," he said, starting towards the right-hand path.

"You're most welcome." Player gave a bow, twirling a hand as he did so. "An actor's insight is often disregarded, I find…"

His words died as something uncoiled from the shadows behind, a faint scrape of scales on stone causing Player to half turn. It seemed as if the darkness itself reached out to claim him, the body that sprang forth being completely black save for the gleam of light on its smooth, diamond-scaled skin. A flash of colour came as the thing opened its jaws, revealing a glistening red maw spiked at the corners with fangs the length of a sabre. They pierced Player from chest to groin as the beast snapped its jaws closed, venom dripping as it raised him high. The viscous liquid spattered onto the stone below, birthing smoking honeycomb marks wherever it fell.

Player failed to die despite the fangs speared through his form, struggling manically as the snake raised him up, a roar of agony and rage erupting from his mask. Hissing, it shook him, snake and prey blurring with sufficient violence to dislodge his mask. It spun down to clatter onto the walkway at Pilgrim's feet. For a second his gaze was captured by the blank eye sockets, then another cry of pain drew his gaze back to the ugly spectacle above.

I told you, the voice said with a self-satisfied note of triumph as Pilgrim took in the sight of Player's revealed face. His skin was a dark, mottled shade of crimson set in a snarl of agonised fury that revealed a set of elongated, sharp pointed teeth. His eyes were a dull shade of yellow beneath a brow riven by small, horn-like protrusions.

"Demon!" Pilgrim heard Book exclaim in shock before the huge snake vanished back into the shadows, taking its prize with it.

◆━━◆

"You knew what he was, didn't you?" Maisha asked Pilgrim as he carried her along the walkway. Her strength had given out an hour before, causing her to sit down with a muttered request that they leave her. Instead, he had stooped to gather her into his arms and bore her on, ignoring her thinly voiced protestations. "Player, I mean to say," she added with a cough.

"I suspected," he said. "The Crucible's blow should have killed him. And, however skilled he might have been with that crossbow, it was unlikely a high-status Arethian fop could have survived a journey all the way from his city to the Execration."

"Makes one wonder what his mission might have been here." She coughed again and allowed her head to loll against his shoulder. "After all, what manner of demon is given to prayer?"

"Perhaps he didn't come to pray at all."

A soft scraping sound came from the shadows to the right and he turned in time to catch sight of a huge, elongated body uncoiling from one pillar to wrap itself around another. The snake, surely the most monstrous of the Mad God's pets, had kept pace with them since claiming Player. Book, speaking in tones of forced, near-hysterical humour, had wondered aloud if the demon had failed to sate its appetite, but they all knew that what drove the beast was not hunger, but malice. They had greeted its first few appearances by brandishing their shards of kraken bone, to which it appeared indifferent, although it hadn't yet chosen to make another attack.

"What will you pray for?" Maisha asked him, raising her half-lidded gaze with a weak smile before subsiding into another bout of coughing. This time he saw blood on her lips when the hacking finally abated.

"Stay with us," he murmured, putting his lips close to her ear, "and I'll pray for you."

"No." Her head lolled from side to side. "Don't waste it. Without my husband, I have no reason to pray for life. A life without him…" Her gaze grew distant and she rested her head on his chest once more. "We risked all coming here, but then our love had always been a risk. Do you know of the Allied Ports? The castes that bind them?"

"I know alchemists are of the second highest caste," he said. "Only the Treasurers stand higher."

"A well-travelled man, I see." She shuddered and he feared another trial of coughs but she settled and spoke on. "Yes, I was born to a family of alchemists. Great was our renown and our wealth. Great enough to require a small army of guards, men of the Sword Caste. It's a middle rank in the ports, but well respected. Still, they are only permitted to talk to the higher ranks when spoken to." Her smile became wistful, but also sad. "And, from the moment I set eyes on the man my father had set to guard my workshop, I took every opportunity to make him talk to me. Caste may have bound us, but love breaks all bonds. Love between castes is forbidden on pain of death, but we feared separation more. And so we fled. Even though it dishonoured our families, disgraced us for all time. We fled as far as we could, all the way to the eastern shore of the Fifth Sea. My family, however, has a very long reach."

His gaze roamed over her face, seeing only a faint echo of statuesque beauty beneath the waxy, hollowed mask. "They did this to you," he said.

Her shoulders moved in a shrug. "Honour required it."

"Did you take vengeance?"

"To what end? There is no cure. My husband raged, of course, as men will. I salved his need for retribution with a quest, an old fable I'd heard about a maddened god who grants wishes. I always knew it was folly, but he needed this, he needed to do...something."

"Should I escape this place," Pilgrim promised her, "I will be your vengeance."

"I'm no seer, but I sense you have exacted enough of that in your time." Her eyes flicked to the sword handle jutting above his shoulder. "That was not crafted by a human hand, and you detest it. I see it in your face every time you draw it. That is why you came here."

He saw Priest raise a hand as they came to a more brightly lit stretch of walkway, bringing them to a halt. The additional illumination came from an opening at its far end through which Pilgrim could make out a trickle of daylight, revealing an expanse of stone so pockmarked it resembled the vast abandoned hive of unfeasibly large hornets. Looking up, the reason became obvious. The cavern roof above was riven with numerous holes, each wide enough to allow passage of a huge snake. Their irregular edges indicated they had been crafted over the course of many years by a near-constant drip of caustic venom.

"To step upon that is death," Seeker stated flatly, her eyes lingering on the holes above. "It's waiting."

Maisha went into another round of coughing, the worst yet, her heaving so violent Pilgrim was forced to set her body down lest she wrest herself from his arms. "My pack," she gasped. "I have something...to banish the pain."

He unslung the pack from his shoulder and handed it to her, turning to the others as they bickered over their options.

"Why not just run across?" Book suggested.

"You've seen how swiftly it moves," Seeker said. "We can't hope to outrun it."

"Perhaps," his tongue emerged to lick at sweat-salted lips, "if we all ran as one. It—" his tongue licked again as his bright, moistened eyes flicked between their faces. "It can't get us all."

"Then you won't object to going first," she suggested, with a pointed glance ahead.

"I, ah, don't run so fast. Why not," his throat constricted in a hard swallow as he nodded at Chena, "send it first. As bait, I mean to say."

"Shut your craven fucking mouth," Seeker instructed. "I mean to say."

"It goes against all sense to favour the life of a dumb beast over our own…"

He fell to an abrupt silence as Pilgrim stepped forward, clamping a hand on his fleshy shoulder. "There is some sense in your words," he said, taking a firmer grip, "regarding bait."

Terror warred with a palpable hatred on Book's face as Pilgrim began to propel him towards the pockmarked stone. The Risen priest's lips worked like overactive slugs as he began to babble, but whether he intended to beg or spit defiance, Pilgrim would never know.

Maisha's feet made a scrabbling sound as she hurried onto the honeycomb surface of the walkway, a bright flurry of sparks rising from the wick set into the apple-sized iron sphere she held. She moved with a spastic, jerky energy that told of a soul battling immense pain, but somehow she was smiling when she came to a halt. She turned to Pilgrim as she raised the sparkling sphere above her head. "No vengeance!" she called to him, and it seemed to him all her beauty returned in that moment, her smile being so bright. "Promise me!"

Any answer he might have given died as the snake descended from the hole directly above her, jaws widening and closing with such reflexive swiftness it all seemed to happen before he had time to register the fact of her demise. The explosion came as the snake recoiled, its mighty head vanishing in a nova of ichor and flame. The body, writhing and coiling, slipped from the hole to collide with the walkway before tumbling into the void below, leaving only a thin pall of smoke and pools of ichor to mark its passing.

Chapter Eight

THE GLASS SEA

•)————(•)————(•

"I t's so…" Seeker blinked in baffled wonder as she gazed at the curved monolith rising in the distance. "Big," she finished with a sardonic grin that faded quickly as she turned to regard Pilgrim's unyielding visage.

The Supplicants' Path had conveyed them onto a ledge overlooking a plain that stretched away towards the Crescent for a distance of at least a dozen miles, and still the temple of the Mad God appeared so immense as to defy understanding. It sat upon a perfectly circular island separated from the plain by a waterless moat, spanned by a single bridge. The Crescent seemed to balance atop the island with unnatural precision, a massive pointed stone curve of impossible architecture that could only be the work of a divine hand. The plain that surrounded it was almost as difficult to comprehend, a vast, dark expanse that resembled the frozen waves of an ocean in the way its uneven surface caught the light. Yet Pilgrim found no wonder in it, no sense of awe. Maisha's face before the snake's jaws closed on her lingered in his mind with a clarity that refused to fade. *No vengeance,* she had said. He knew she meant it kindly, a release from any obligation he would harbour towards her memory, but for him it felt like a curse.

Quite so, my liege, the voice piped up. *For without vengeance, what are you?*

"She was a good woman," Seeker told him. "But chose her own end and met it well. A death to be honoured. A memory to be cherished." He knew that her people were not given to overt expressions of sympathy, in fact children born to the beast charmer clans were punished for it. So this, he knew, must be hard for her.

"Only one more day's journey," he said, nodding at the Crescent. "And your prayer will be heard."

"If he chooses to hear it. He may find yours just as worthy."

"I doubt worthiness has much to do with it," Book said. He kept his features as inexpressive as possible, but an accusatory glare shone through whenever he looked at Pilgrim, causing the voice to repeat a frequent observation.

Why do you allow him to live? it asked. *You risk too much for the pleasure of watching the Mad God's cruelties. And what guarantee do you have the crazed loon will kill him in any case? Do it now, my liege.*

"This way," Priest said, making for a set of weathered stone steps carved into the ledge's westward flank. Pilgrim inclined his head at Book and gestured for him to go ahead, which he did after another poorly concealed glare of hatred.

The sky grew dark with cloud by the time they descended the stairs to step upon the dark surface of the plain, bringing a stiff wind seeded with rain. It added to the notion of the ground before them being some kind of petrified sea. The surface was formed of a hard black crystal that rose and fell as it stretched away on either side, in some places shaped into facsimiles of cresting waves or swirling currents. Pilgrim found it hard to credit this as the work of the elements, a suspicion confirmed by Priest as they began their trek across the tract of windswept glass.

"Once this was a vast mirror of obsidian," he said. "Crafted by the Absolved as a perfect reflection of the heavens. For centuries, not a crack nor a scratch marred its surface no matter how many supplicants strode across it. After the fall it became this. None know why, but it's thought he could no longer tolerate the sight of perfection and so rendered it into a storm-tossed sea."

"Perfection is an impossibility," Book said, a quotation from the Injunctions of the First Risen. "It is through our imperfections that we come to know ourselves."

"Then," Seeker told him, "you must know yourself very well."

Rain began to fall in earnest as the sky disappeared behind a thick veil of cloud. Lacking shelter, they had no option but to wrap their cloaks tight about them and forge on across the jagged plain. Soon lightning joined the gale and the deluge, completing the sense of being adrift in a maelstrom far from land.

"Do you think he knows we're coming?" Seeker shouted above the wind's howl.

Pilgrim squinted at the Crescent, now just an immense shadow against the drifting clouds save for the flashes of lightning that sent brief sheets of luminescence across its flanks. The sword gave a discomforted thrum as he strode on, though the voice stayed silent. He discerned a brooding quality to it the closer they drew to their goal, as if it were lost in unwelcome contemplation. Whatever awaited them in the Crescent, the voice evidently did not relish the meeting.

After a prolonged trek, during which the storm swelled and waned several times, he saw Priest come to an abrupt halt in the lee of a tall frozen wave. A flash of lightning lit the comparatively flat stretch of glass beyond, revealing a large number of what appeared to be human figures. The storm calmed again as he came to Priest's side, the clouds thinning a little to allow daylight to play over several hundred people. They were all skeletally thin and mostly naked save for the rags that clung to a few. Some wandered in aimless circles with heads bowed, others strode back and forth, gesticulating with animated urgency. Most simply stood and stared at the Crescent. But all, without exception, were speaking.

"More dritch-wights?" Book wondered, surveying the multitude.

"Wights don't talk," Priest said. His brow was set in a frown of grim understanding as he started forward once more, approaching the nearest figure without apparent fear. It was a man, tall with the vestiges of once-impressive muscles still clinging to his bones. He stood naked upon the glass, repeatedly raising his arms to the crescent as he voiced the same request over and over.

"Please, return to me my son. Please, return to me my son..."

He paid no heed to Priest as the cleric paused in scrutiny, continuing his mantra, gaze never straying from the shadowed bulk of the Crescent. Priest bowed his head in momentary sorrow before gesturing for them to follow as he turned and resumed the trek. Pilgrim glanced at the tall man as he passed by, seeing a bearded, wide-eyed face oblivious to anything save his endless question. They passed a woman next, young and partially clad in the remnants of once-fine clothes reduced to mildewed rags. She moved in a ragged circle, hands clutching at her belly and face formed into an ugly rictus as she spoke through gritted teeth.

"My child deserved to be born. My bitch sister had a child. Why was mine taken from my womb? Give her back to me..."

Next a young man speaking a language beyond Pilgrim's knowledge, but the stricken expression and anguish on his face spoke of a love lost or unrequited. Beyond him an old woman on her knees, her hands clasped for so long they seemed to have fused together as she begged for the death of the mistress her husband had abandoned her for. The voices merged as they pressed on, a discordant chorus of desperate entreaties voiced in a dozen tongues. "My father's birthright... The treasure should have been mine... I ask only for justice... They call me mad, make me sane... Take away every memory of her..."

Priest halted once more as the crowd thinned. Only a few hundred paces away lay the bridge across the moat, guarded by a large gate flanked by two tall pillars. However, Priest's gaze was focused entirely on the face of a man with a long mane of white hair. Unlike every other unfortunate they had passed, this one was silent. He was also clothed, although his garments were tattered and would soon slough away. Even so, Pilgrim recognised his threadbare cloak as being identical to the one worn by Priest.

"Prelate," the young cleric said, greeting the silent man with a formal bow of his head. The man gave no response, his face upturned to the tallest of the Crescent's points. Pilgrim could see no mania in his eyes, only anger touched by a deep, unquenchable sadness.

"Prelate," Priest repeated, reaching out to grasp the man's arm. "I must know, did you pray?"

The man blinked his eyes slowly before focusing them on Priest. His lips parted with a dry rasp and the voice that emerged was a hollow thing, void of emotion save for a clear note of bitterness. "I prayed," he said. "I beseeched his return to those who love and worship him. I begged for the restoration of these lands and the release of the benighted souls who dwell here. He...laughed at me, brother."

The old priest blinked again, angling his head as his brow formed a quizzical frown. "Now...I pray for death. Will you kill me?"

Priest's hand slipped from the man's sleeve, his face white as he retreated and turned away, deaf to his prelate's softly spoken plea. "A year I've waited...is it too much to ask from a brother in faith?" He reached out to Priest's retreating back, but the awareness on his face faded quickly and his arm slipped to his side. He resumed his vigil, paying no heed to Pilgrim or the others as they passed by.

Priest approached the gate with a determined stride, unfastening his cloak and casting it away. He continued to strip when he halted, casting off his shirt to stand bare-chested in front of the thick iron bars that filled the portal. The bars were set within an arch of white marble, metal and stone free of any sign of age or weathering. The pillars on either side of the gate were similarly unmarred, the relief carvings that marked them from base to top appearing to have been crafted only days before. The sky had darkened again, bringing a resurgence of the storm and Pilgrim's view of the carvings came via the lightning that flashed overhead. The pillars were similar in many ways to the tall columns he had seen in Valkeris, echoing the same precision and skill in the execution of the carvings. However,

Valkerin columns were invariably martial in nature, phalanxes of legionaries subduing an endless procession of barbarian tribes. These were different, depicting scenes of joy rather than war. Smiling, laughing people gathered harvests or constructed tall buildings. Others danced and frolicked in carnal abandon amidst a bounteous feast. These then had been the people of Alnachim, or at least a preserved testament to how their god chose to remember his adherents.

"I come as a supplicant to the Absolved!" Priest intoned, drawing Pilgrim's gaze back to the gate. He stood with his arms raised, his bared torso streaming with rain as the sky unleashed a fresh torrent. "Know that I have borne all burdens, suffered all punishments!" Priest turned to present his back to the gate and Pilgrim saw the many scars that marred it. Some were old, others standing out as fresh, livid red stripes across his skin. It was clear he had been whipped regularly since childhood. "Bear witness to my suffering and know that it was accepted gladly for every stroke brought me closer to this day. To seek the blessing of the Absolved is to recognise his suffering and join with it."

He paused to take a small knife from his belt, putting the edge to his palm and drawing blood before approaching the gate, hand outstretched. "By virtue of suffering endured and blood freely given," he said, pressing his bloody palm to one of the bars, "I seek communion with the Absolved!"

"Pilgrim," Seeker said. Her voice was faint amidst the storm, but the urgency in it undeniable. She had one of her few remaining arrows nocked to her bowstring, rain-streaked brow furrowed as she focused on the denizens of the glass sea. Pilgrim saw that they were all still now, the aimless pacing or circling replaced by immobility. Also, despite the continuing thunder he could tell they had fallen silent, their gazes uniformly fixed on the gate with hungry expectation.

"Their prayers were denied," Book said, backing away. "But still they seek the Mad God's blessing."

The grind of metal on stone snapped Pilgrim's gaze to the gate to see the iron barrier ascending with an irksome slowness. Book crouched at its base, casting wary glances at the undying pilgrims as they started forward. They were hesitant at first, taking a few tottering steps, but as the bars rose ever higher their compulsion to have their prayers answered took hold and they began to run.

Pilgrim drew the sword, the handle vibrating in his hand. Hearing a desperate groaning, he turned to see Book scrambling under the slowly ascending gate, teeth gritted as he attempted to force his bulk through the gap.

"Go," Pilgrim told Priest. "Best if he's not allowed to proceed alone. We'll follow."

The cleric nodded and lowered himself to the ground, crawling under the gate with markedly more ease than Book. "You next," Pilgrim said to Seeker. The crowd of denied suppliants were only thirty paces off now, and closing fast.

"Not without Chena," she stated, loosing her arrow into the oncoming crowd. He saw one body fall, speared through the neck, but couldn't tell if it lay still amongst the confusion of the onrushing throng. Chena stood close to her mistress, hackles raised and yapping in challenge.

"I'll guard her," he said. "Go."

It was as he jerked his head at the gate that he heard the snick of a spring and the scrape of steel on wood. Turning, he saw Book rising to a crouch, his thumb pressed to a knot in the wood of his staff. A foot-long length of sharpened steel emerged in a flash from the base of the staff, stabbing into Priest's bare chest as he got to his knees. The cleric convulsed as the blade pierced him, jutting through to his spine. Pilgrim saw Book grimace with unaccustomed distaste as he twisted the blade to make sure before drawing it free, allowing Priest to collapse lifeless to the ground.

"By virtue of suffering endured," Book said, crouching to press his hand to the gushing wound in Priest's back before rushing to the gate and smearing it onto the bars, "and blood freely given!"

Pilgrim lunged as the barrier crashed down with a sound like a tolling bell. He thrust the sword through the bars but Book, moving with a swiftness he hadn't displayed at any point in their journey, jerked aside before the point found his chest.

"You think I don't know who you are?!" the Risen priest spat, brandishing his bloody staff-blade as he backed away. "Whatever vile sorcery you employed to endure all these years didn't fool me! You think I would allow any chance the Mad God would hear your prayer, Ravager?"

He turned and ran across the bridge, shouting hate-filled invective. "Stay and die at the hands of heretics! A deserved end for the worst of tyrants!"

Hearing Chena's yapping turn into a feral growl accompanied by another snap of Seeker's bowstring, Pilgrim whirled. The sword glowed as it swung in a wide arc, slicing through chest and skull to leave a half dozen supplicants on the ground. They twitched and writhed, but failed to die, one still reaching for him with clawed hands despite the brains spilling from his skull.

"Back!" Pilgrim said, pushing Seeker away from the gate and towards the pillar on the right. With her last arrow gone she abandoned her bow and drew her scimitar, both of them hacking their way clear of the encroaching mob. Despite the many lopped limbs and shattered skulls the wretched souls continued to assail them, Pilgrim and Seeker finding their backs pressed against the pillar's base. He swung the sword with all the demonic force he could summon from its occupant, the voice singing with involuntary exultation as it scythed down one ragged body after another. But there were many more, all now screaming out their prayers in an insane cacophony of desperate need.

"I need room!" he shouted to Seeker above the din.

"To do what?" she shouted back.

He lashed at the frenzied supplicants before him with furious energy, creating a brief fountain of limbs and entrails as he forged enough space to allow him to turn to the pillar. "To build a bridge," he said, steadying himself as he drew back the blade. It began to glow brighter still as he conveyed his intention to the voice, provoking a reflective chuckle.

Something I've never seen done, my liege, it said. *I do like it when you attempt the impossible.*

Seeker seemed to sense his purpose, launching herself at the mob with renewed vigour whilst Chena charged forward, her mighty jaws snapping at the forest of legs, crushing bone like paper. The respite they created was brief, barely a few seconds, but it was all he needed.

Pilgrim swung the sword when the blade's glow had blossomed to a near-blinding white. The first stroke sliced through the fine carvings like an axe cleaving the flimsiest wood. The second bit deeper still, the huge monolith beginning to totter. It fell with the third stroke, severed from its base in a cloud of powdered stone, toppling over so that its summit slammed onto the ground opposite, spanning the moat. The impact birthed a series of cracks along its entire length and Pilgrim surmised their newly crafted bridge would last only moments.

"Go!" he instructed Seeker, cutting down a supplicant who had managed to grab hold of her scimitar blade.

"Chena!" she called to the hyena, now deep in the ranks of the mob. She reared up, latching her jaws onto the neck of a supplicant and crushing the spine. She cast the body away and began to claw her way towards Seeker, jaws snapping, long-nailed paws slashing. But the throng was too thick, several hands latching onto her pelt, halting her progress whilst others leapt on her back to bear her down.

Seeker let out a feral cry of anguish as the supplicants tore at Chena's thrashing form, her snarls soon becoming piteous and plaintive whimpers. Seeker started forward, slashing wildly with her scimitar even as the beast's cries dwindled and died.

"No." Pilgrim caught Seeker about the waist, bearing her towards the pillar. "She's gone."

Seeker struggled in his grip, drawing her scimitar back to stab at his eyes, but then stopping at his implacable, almost judgemental stare. "Your daughter," was all he said. It was enough.

She nodded and he released her, pushing her ahead as they started along the pillar to the far side. Fresh cracks appeared in the monolith's surface as they ran, adding further ruin to its joyous carvings. Pilgrim felt the great mass of stone begin to crumble when they were still several paces from the end and shouted at Seeker to jump, following her a heartbeat later. The pillar came apart whilst he was still in the air, the summit subliming into fragments as his midriff connected with the island's edge. His purchase on the smooth surface was meagre and he would most likely have followed the pillar into the chasm if Seeker hadn't leapt to grip his arm, arresting his fall long enough for his foot to find a toehold and push him to safety.

They lay side by side, panting in the rain as it subsided into a faint drizzle. When Pilgrim gathered strength enough to get to his feet he saw the supplicants on the other side drifting away in apparent indifference. With their chance of regaining the Mad God's attention gone, it seemed their cursed state reasserted itself. Within moments their discordant chorus rose once more, hundreds of disappointed souls begging to a god too uncaring or mad to hear them.

"I intend to take my time with that treacherous fuck," Seeker said, taking Pilgrim's proffered hand to haul herself upright. "I trust that won't be a problem."

They both turned to the tall black rectangle that formed the entrance to the Crescent as a loud and very long scream sounded from within.

"I doubt either of us have a say in his fate now," Pilgrim said, starting forward.

Chapter Nine

THE
MAD GOD

•)———(•)———(•

"How does it go again? Be so good as to remind me."

"A g-good man hath no need of…of riches, only… only the company of souls worthy of his g-goodness."

The voices echoed through the cavernous interior of the Crescent, softly spoken but clearly audible. Book's halting, agonised tones were easily recognised as he stumbled his way through a recitation of Risen scripture. The other voice was surprising in its humanity, lacking the unnatural resonance Pilgrim expected.

"Yes," it said, faint with reflection. "That was it. Tell me, are *you* a good man?"

"I-I…serve the Church of the Risen…"

"I'll take that as a no."

The scream was the loudest yet, a familiar high-pitched shriek that only came from burning. It lasted long enough for Pilgrim and Seeker to make their way from the entrance and into a matrix of diagonal pillars. He gestured for her to stop at the sight of an expanse of bare stone ahead. It lacked any features. No statues, no throne for the Mad God to sit upon. Just a long avenue empty save for the two figures in its centre. Above them rose the complex mesh of beams and pillars that kept this impossible structure in being. Pilgrim assumed the way even softly spoken voices echoed effortlessly through it all must be a deliberate artefact of its design.

To Pilgrim's surprise, Book was on his feet rather than lying in a crumpled state on the floor. From the way his sagging, terrorised features stared at the black-robed man standing a few feet away, it was clear he was being kept upright by virtue of another's will. Book's arms were outstretched, smoke rising from the swirling red marks in his flesh, the scent of charred meat pervading the air with sickening sweetness.

"The First Advisory of the Second Risen," said the man in the black robe after a moment's contemplation. He was tall but not excessively so, his frame athletic but not mighty. He wore a peppercorn beard on a face that appeared to be that of a handsome man in early middle age, his black hair streaked with silver swept back from a smooth forehead. His robe was plain and he wore no regalia of any kind. "I always liked that one," he added, flicking a hand at Book.

"A w-wise man…" Book choked as he coughed the words out, spittle flying from his lips as he tried not to retch at the stench of his own burnt flesh, "doth not look…" He paused, swallowing hard, features bunching in terrorised anticipation, "…look to gods for succour or…s-salvation…" He tried to speak on but his terror overtook him, leaving him shuddering as piss flooded the floor around his feet.

"No salvation from gods, eh?" the man in the black robe repeated, lips pursed and eyebrows raised. "I can't say I disagree with that one. In fact," he stepped closer to Book, frowning as he inspected his face, "I think it so important it should be inscribed upon your very skull, my faithful friend."

Pilgrim had expected to enjoy the sight of Book's demise, but, as the glowing red letters appeared on his balding pate, burning their way down to the bone beneath as he shrieked his lungs empty, he found it pitiful. The scale of the man's delusion had been colossal, to think he could pray a being like this out of existence. He was more a mad man than a fanatic, and the mad should be pitied, however well deserved their end.

The voice spoke up as Book spasmed and died, still held upright by the Mad God's will. *Are you getting sentimental, my liege?*

Book's body flew away as the man in the black robe focused his gaze on the spot where Pilgrim and Seeker crouched behind a pillar. "Come out!" the Mad God commanded. "I would know who has brought an exile into my domain."

Well, the voice sighed as Pilgrim stepped into view. *This is awkward.*

The man in the black robe spared Pilgrim a brief glance before fixing his eyes on the sword on his back. "Hello, Lakorath," he said.

My lord, the voice replied.

The Mad God beckoned them closer, Pilgrim seeing little option but to comply. Seeker followed a few steps behind as he approached, halting a few paces from the pool of piss left by Book. Glancing to the right, Pilgrim saw the Risen priest's body crumpled into the base of a pillar, smoke still rising from the letters seared into his scalp.

"One of the seven cursed blades," the Mad God said, Pilgrim turning back to see his gaze still fixed on the sword.

He gave a small shake of his head accompanied by a minuscule laugh. "So, this was your fate when the Triumvirate banished you from the Infernus. I would find it pitiable if it hadn't been so richly deserved."

I assure you the price of my transgressions has been paid in full, the voice replied. *Many times over.*

"And yet you remain locked within that trinket and in thrall to this mortal." The Mad God's eyes flicked to Pilgrim in contempt. "Or did you somehow contrive to trick him into coming here? Were you so keen to renew our acquaintance?"

I didn't know who exactly the Mad God was until this moment. I suspected you might be a demon of the Second or Third Circle. To find the greatest warlord of the First Circle here is shocking, I must say. Did they exile you too, I wonder?

The Mad God's face twitched in faint annoyance. "Don't test me, Lakorath. Millennia may have passed but my regard for you has not changed."

Pilgrim felt the sword shift on his back, as if squirming. He took considerable note of the fact that the voice remained silent.

"You," the Mad God snapped, looking again at Pilgrim. "I assume you came to beg for something. What is it?"

Pilgrim exchanged a glance with Seeker. "We both came to pray," he said. "Our prayers are different…"

"They always are." The Mad God gave a weary shake of his head and wandered away from them, hands clasped behind his back as he moved to stand over Book's corpse. "This one, in his insane arrogance, imagined all he had to do in order to banish me from this world was to spout some doggerel from his church's scripture. As if I had never heard it before, as if it hadn't been the spell that woke me from my own delusions.

"Centuries ago their missionaries came to my kingdom to spread their vapid attempts at wisdom, and it actually took hold. Those who had been my worshippers, had enjoyed lives of plenty and peace under my benevolence, chose instead to worship the words of those who pretended to have risen from the dead. It…angered me, enraged me in fact. So I made unto their missionaries a gift of their own scripture, searing it into their bones so that they could never escape it. A necessarily fatal process, but when it was done, when I had scourged all traces of their heresy from my dominion, I found that my rage had cured me. The centuries I had spent here were a lie, the work of a maddened demon who imagined himself a god, now made sane. Didn't you find that to be the case?" he asked, turning back to Pilgrim. "Didn't your rage cure you of the delusion of love, Ravager?"

He smiled, moving away from Book's body as he approached Pilgrim, his steps slow and carefully paced. "Yes, I know you. The legend of King Guyime, Ravager of the Northlands, has even made its way here. Decades ago, a few pilgrims came begging for your death. I denied them, finding you far too entertaining. Now, here you stand, come to implore me to get that sword off your back, despite the unnatural span of years it has given you and all the wonderful things you did with it."

His smile broadened when Pilgrim said nothing. "Didn't you know you travelled with a monster?" the Mad God asked, turning to Seeker. "Did he entertain you along the way with tales of his massacres? The innocents slaughtered whenever his host took a stronghold or captured a city. And the purges, of course. All those Risen priests flayed, scourged and burnt at his order. By the time it was over, when thousands lay dead, he had made himself the greatest king the northlands had ever known, whereupon he promptly disappeared. Have you been trying to rid yourself of the sword all this time, Your Highness? I can't say I blame you. Lakorath was always very trying company."

His gaze narrowed as it lingered on Seeker. Her monochrome painted features tensed under his scrutiny, eyes tracking to Pilgrim, either in judgement or disbelief, he couldn't tell. "And you have a long-lost relative to find," the Mad God said, frowning in concentration. "A daughter, apparently. Stolen by slavers whilst you were off finding new beasts to make friends with. Not a very good mother, are you?"

"I have atonement to make," she replied, voice hoarse but steady. "And I'll make it once I've recovered her."

"How pathetically noble of you."

Pilgrim saw the demon in him then, the glint of cruelty in his eyes, the slight predatory snarl that revealed teeth that seemed sharper than they should. The Mad God was neither mad nor a god. He was a fully sane demon with an endless supply of victims to feed his cruelty.

"But your prayer is too mundane," he said, waving a dismissive hand. "You will join my chorus on the glass sea, another note of sorrow to delight my ears. Whilst your prayer, King Guyime," his smile broadened as he regarded Pilgrim, "I am more than willing to grant."

"I pray for her," Pilgrim said, stepping in front of Seeker. "Restore her daughter. If you will answer but one prayer, let it be hers."

"Oh, don't be tiresome." The Mad God's smile became a wince. "I have little patience for those who pretend heroism. And it really doesn't suit you."

"No, it doesn't," Pilgrim agreed. "Yes, they called me the Ravager, dread king of the northlands, persecutor of the Risen church. They killed my wife, called her a whore and a heretic, tied her to a stake and burnt her alive because she held to the forest gods of her people. And I made them pay. I left a trail of blood and slaughter a thousand miles long..." He faltered, the truth somehow catching his throat, truth he had never spoken, even to himself. "But it was never the sword," he went on, forcing the words out. "Yes, I sought out a demon-cursed blade and used it to win my battles and kill my enemies, but I wielded it, it never wielded me. I earned this bondage and more besides. I do not pray for me, I pray for her."

The Mad God raised an amused eyebrow. "You think this redeems you? It is but the merest grain on a scale that will never balance. History will always name you the Ravager."

"History will." Pilgrim nodded at Seeker, now half crouched, ready to run or fight, not that either would avail them anything. "But she won't. I pray for her. Restore this woman's daughter."

The Mad God's hands made a soft, percussive slap as he slowly clapped them together, the sound somehow contriving to echo throughout the vastness of the Crescent. "Marvellous," he said, letting his hands fall to his side. "How sad our scholarly friend over there isn't alive to write it down."

His smile abruptly disappeared and, in the space of an eye-blink, all trace of humanity slipped from his face. Pilgrim could see shades of this thing's true nature roiling beneath its skin, thorn-like spines rising, the muscles of its neck bulging as two small, growing red dots appeared in its eyes, burning like coals in a furnace.

"Do you imagine there are rules here, mortal?" he enquired in a voice that combined an animalistic growl with a rush of heated air. "Your kind summoned me from the Infernus in the midst of my madness and made me their god, thinking they had cleansed me of my nature, naming me the Absolved in their naivety." He advanced towards them, his voice building as he spoke in time with each step. "They…made…me…into…an ABOMINATION!"

Pilgrim was forced to shield his face from the blast of air that accompanied his final shout, hot enough to blister the back of his hand.

"This is my domain," the Mad God continued, his eyes burning now and flame licking around his lips. "Subject to *my* wants, *my* desires. I desire a new voice for my chorus and I desire your sword. I'll sunder it from you, as you wish. Lakorath can serve me once more, as he did in the Infernus. And you, Your Highness, can take the place of my Crucible. You killed him so it seems only fair. Pilgrims will still come, regardless of whether any remnant remains of the Church of the Absolved. They will walk beneath your gaze and you will judge them. Won't you enjoy that? It's what you were always good at, after all."

A shrill, desperate cry came from the voice then, all surety and humour stripped away and replaced by simple terror and panic. *Kill him! I'll not be his slave again! KILL HIM!*

It seemed to leap into his hand as he reached for it, the blade like a curtain of white fire as he brought it down, intending to cleave the Mad God from crown to crotch. It was like striking an anvil, the blade rebounding from its target without leaving as much as a scratch.

The Mad God smiled and delivered a single jab of his finger to Pilgrim's chest. He flew from his feet as if struck by a warhammer, landing hard and sliding across the smooth marble of the floor to collide with the forest of slanted pillars. Too stunned to move, he could only watch as Seeker drew her scimitar and launched herself at the Mad God, screaming in challenge. He laughed as he swatted her aside, sending her into a high overhead tumble to impact on the marble twenty paces away.

"Now, Your Highness," the Mad God said, advancing towards Pilgrim with a brisk, purposeful stride. "Time to educate you in your new responsi-"

His words died as something very fast flickered at the edge of Pilgrim's vision. The Mad God let out a flaming roar of pain, sinking to his knees and reaching for the crossbow bolt embedded in his shoulder. A whirring sound drew Pilgrim's gaze to the Crescent's entrance. Player had regained both his mask and his crossbow, and stood working the windlass of the latter with inhuman speed, sliding the string into the lock and slotting a fresh bolt in place in the space of mere seconds. He trained it on the Mad God as he roared again, struggling to his feet. The second bolt slammed into his uninjured shoulder with sufficient force to send him onto his back.

Player reloaded the crossbow with the same unnatural rapidity as he advanced to stand over the Mad God's writhing form. He stared up at the masked figure with his burning eyes blazing hatred, spitting curses in a language Pilgrim had never heard but sent a jolt of pain through him with every word.

Demon tongue, the voice told him. *Not meant for mortal ears, my liege. Mortals don't react well to it.*

The Mad God's defiance transformed into a roaring scream as Player methodically loosed two more bolts into each of his legs. Player spoke then, employing the same pain-inducing tongue, the voice translating for Pilgrim's benefit.

"Thine tenure in the mortal realm is decreed over," Player informed the Mad God. "The balance hath tipped, and must be restored."

The four bolts speared into the Mad God's flesh began to glow then, bright points of light blossoming then exuding tendrils of shimmering energy that instantly joined together, creating a fiery cage.

"Thou..." the Mad God grated, flames pouring from his mouth and nostrils, "hath not the rank..."

"The Triumvirate commands me." Player reloaded the crossbow once more and trained it on the prostrate demon's head. "Punishment awaits thee in the Infernus."

The bolt slammed into the Mad God's forehead, whereupon his body took on a trembling rictus. The final bolt blossomed and soon joined its infernal energy to the others, Pilgrim seeing a dark shimmer spread across the floor beneath the twitching body. It was vague at first but soon deepened, the edges hardening to create a portal through which Pilgrim could see distant fires burning.

Player stepped close to the edge of the portal, removing his mask as he turned to regard Pilgrim. The demonic features were even more misshapen than when first revealed. A series of large pustules marred his faced from check to neck, the depredations of the snake's venom Pilgrim supposed.

"It spat me out," Player explained with a grimace. "I wasn't to its taste." He gave one of his florid bows, speaking in much the same theatrical tones as before, though his voice had gained a good deal of depth. "Thank you for leaving my mask. Its glamour concealed my presence in his domain, you see."

"You are very much welcome," Pilgrim assured him in a groan, getting painfully to his feet. "Tell me," he said. "Was there ever a real Player?"

"Oh, yes indeed. A famously inept Arethian actor with a foolish notion of making pilgrimage to the Execration to beseech the Mad God for the talent he craved. I made him a better bargain. Now, he plays to very appreciative audiences in a performance that never ends." Player inclined his head at the portal and the distant fires below. "In there, where I must now return."

He started forward but paused again. "The seven cursed blades were set upon the earth for a purpose," he said. "To release the demons that dwell within them, that purpose must be fulfilled, for that they must be brought together." He gave Pilgrim a grave smile. "If you still wish to be freed from it, that is."

He turned his gaze on the shuddering form of the Mad God and sighed as he laid his hand upon it, muttering in the demon tongue, "They should have allowed me to extinguish thee, my lord. Thou were as much blight upon our realm as theirs."

They fell then, disappearing into the portal in a blaze of near-blinding energy. Pilgrim averted his eyes, blinking tears until he saw only a bare marble floor and no sign of either demon.

"What was he?" Pilgrim asked the voice. "The Mad God, in the Infernus."

A demon lord of the First Circle, also a warrior and general of great renown. Demons do love to war with one another, and he loved it more than any other. I was his most trusted spy, for a time. It didn't last.

"His name?"

Best left unspoken.

Pilgrim went to Seeker, finding her stunned and barely conscious. A loud and ominous crack from above, followed by a cascade of dust, convinced him to gather her up and hurry towards the exit. The Crescent began to crumble before he carried her free of the structure, dodging falling masonry. He didn't pause when outside, running across the bridge to the gate beyond. The iron bars had been wrenched and bent to create an opening, presumably the result of Player's inhuman strength. Pilgrim ducked through and turned to watch the Crescent collapse into itself as if drawn by some internal fist. Dust billowed in huge clouds as the giant curve toppled and shattered. The destruction seemed to act as a contagion, spreading to the bridge which cracked from end to end before tumbling into the chasm below. The gate and the surviving pillar went next, fragmenting into ever-smaller pieces until they were mere mounds of dust soon to be scattered by the wind.

Pilgrim saw the bodies of the supplicants littering the glass sea, itself rapidly turning to black sand that soon covered them in dunes. The clouds that had shrouded this place parted, allowing sunlight to bathe the newly crafted desert and the mountains beyond. Although it lay far beyond his sight, he knew the City of Spires would also now be turning to dust whilst the dritch-wights and the remnants of the Mad God's menagerie would finally succumb to the rot that was their due.

Seeker groaned and shifted in his arms so he set her down. As she regained her senses the fear on her face quickly turned to sorrow at the sight of the ruin around them, her head sagging in defeat.

"The demon that resides in the blade I carry," he told her, "once guided me to a man I had hunted years before and thought long dead. It hears all lies and knows all tongues. We will find your daughter. The most successful slavers take their captives to the port of Salish where the Fourth Sea meets the Fifth. We'll start there."

"I've been to Salish," she said. "And found no trace of her."

"You haven't been there with me."

She gave a cautious nod, a new wariness in her gaze as she met his. "Was it true?" she asked. "The things he said you did. The name he called you. Ravager."

"All true."

She nodded again and took a breath before getting to her feet. "I think I'll just keep calling you Pilgrim."

"And to me you shall remain Seeker."

He glanced back at the tumbled ruin of the Crescent, feeling a pang of loss at the inscribed skull Book had carried to his death. He had hoped to crush it to powder before this was over.

So, the voice said as they started across the desert of black sand. *You intend to remain a persecutor, my liege?*

"I intend to resume the oath I swore over my wife's burnt corpse," he murmured in reply. "For far too long have I allowed you to distract me. And it occurs to me there's more than one way to destroy a church."

With the seven swords? This world is vast and full of dangers. Do you really think you can find them?

"In addition to its famed slave market, Salish has the finest archive in the Five Seas." He raised his face to the sunlight, enjoying the warmth after days beyond its reach. "It's where I found you, after all."